A mess age

from the

future

If you want to find the secrets of the universe, think in terms of energy, frequency and vibration.
Nikola Tesla

But the day of the Lord will come like a thief, and then the heavens will pass away with a roar, and the heavenly bodies will be burned up and dissolved, and the earth and the works that are done on it will be exposed.

Peter:3.10

Prologue

Berlin, Germany, 1944

Major Hanna sat patiently at his desk. It was quiet now, not like it once was. The hustle and bustle of a once thriving department was long gone. No incessant tap tapping of typists, telephones constantly ringing, footsteps beating hard against the highly polished floor, much to his annoyance. Oh, how he wished things were different. The once multitude of staff was now down to only two, three if you included himself.

Reaching into his drawer he took out a cigarette. He had given up the disgusting habit less than a year ago but now seemed a fitting time to reintroduce his lungs to the acrid smoke they had thought had been banished.

Hanna knew the end was coming. Knew it was hopeless. The Nazi party was falling apart, Germany was falling apart. Indeed, the Fuhrer was falling apart. The great German leader Adolf Hitler was looking more and more to the occult and esoteric teachings rather than battle plans or an escape strategy. The war was over. The great German race will be defeated. Unthinkable only a year ago. Now there was no doubt. Just at a time when the Reich had made some astounding discoveries in fields of science and technology. Now they will all be stolen by the allies who would go on to glory on German discoveries. Still, that was the least of his worries now. Any serving soldier within the German SS was not going to survive this.

As a Major in the SS Space Intelligence Division he had trained as a linguist at the University of Hamburg prior to the war breaking out. At six foot tall, blond, blue eyed, and with a muscular physique, it was obvious to the German high command that Hanna was Aryan. He was superior. He was made for the SS. As the Nazi's became obsessed with myth and legend Hanna had been tasked with more and more bizarre expeditions on behalf of the Fuhrer and Himmler. Spared active service Hanna had never actually fired a live round at the enemy. He had however been chasing Nazi dreams all around the globe including trips to the Amazon rainforest looking for a sacred piece of crystal. A crystal said to have an amazing ability to create massive energy fields. The Sudan to recover the mummified remains of a human believed to be 8 foot tall and over 50,000 years old. An Antarctic expedition where it was said a whole advanced city could be seen buried in the Ice two miles down. This part of Antarctica was re named Neu Schwabenland when he arrived on the orders of Himmler and annexed for the Reich.

All these locations the Nazi's believed were interconnected and would aid Hanna to help them discover their true origins. As Major Hanna savoured the smoke he smiled to himself. All the expeditions had been successful. All of them. And yes he found it difficult to believe it himself sometimes. Each and every one a great success.

The last expedition had also proved that they were all indeed insane. Either that or there was a much bigger conspiracy. One of truly cosmic proportions. He no longer wanted to be a part of it.

All Major Oswald Hanna wanted to do in life was teach. Teach others and further his interest in ancient languages, particularly ancient script and cuneiform text. His protestations at being called up to the Army and then the SS went unacknowledged. And this is where he was now, alone with his secretary and personal driver waiting for an approaching Army.

Carefully, Hanna removed some documents from the open drawer and placed them in an envelope. Taking one last pull on the cigarette he crushed it beneath his foot before sealing the large brown envelope and wring a name on the front. Picking up the telephone receiver he called for his driver. A few moments later his driver, who had been patiently waiting outside, walked in. As the corporal stood to attention in front of Hanna he raised his right arm and ensured a swift but loud connection of his heels. He was loyal to both Germany and Major Hanna.

Hanna stood from behind his desk and walked over to his loyal corporal. He took a moment then extended his hand towards Corporal Scmidt. The corporal stood there whilst Hanna's hand was outstretched, not understanding this unusual situation. Initially resisting he eventually looked Major Hanna in the eye and with his hand still outstretched Corporal Scmidt reached out and took the proffered hand. There was a shake of the hands between both men but no exchange of words. There was a moment when the corporal realised that he may be about to receive his final orders. Major Hanna spoke clearly to the driver and gave him precise instructions before placing the brown envelope in his hand and returned to his desk.

As the driver left the Major's office his secretary knocked and entered. She smiled at the Major as was expected of all good German women who served the Nazi war office. She enquired if he needed anything before his meeting with Himmler. It was scheduled for 4 pm, a little over two hours away. As another loyal servant Anna was expected to keep the Major informed of all his forthcoming meetings for the day and ensure his stress levels were kept to a minimum. It was again expected of all German subordinates to adhere to all their superiors requests. As she approached the desk she looked directly into his eyes and asked, 'Anything else'. Hanna nodded and stood from his seat. Taking the cushion from his seat he dropped it at his feet. Anna smiled, approached and knelt in front of the major. She had done this many times before but it had been a while. She saw it as her duty but one she nonetheless enjoyed very much.

Hanna was married but also had feelings for his secretary who did things that he could not ask his wife to do. There was no love between Major Hanna and the woman kneeling before him but there was a strong bond between them.

Anna never saw the Major reach into the drawer. She never saw the tears in his eyes. She never got to enjoy the Major one last time. She fell backwards, the hole in her temple small on one side but much larger on the other. She would not have heard the bang, he was sure of it. Hanna could not leave her to the mercy of Himmler. She would have suffered, and suffered badly.

Hanna re fastened his trousers, sat down. Took one last look at the family photograph on the desk and calmly placed the luger pistol into his mouth. He tilted it upwards, and fired only his second live round in this war.

Chapter 1

United States, 1954

Colonel Walter 'Walt' Stevens stared at the message on his screen, not fully understanding who had sent it or how it had indeed managed to appear on his television screen.

Message: FAO Colonel Walter Stevens

      US Navy Aerospace Division

Start: 'AT ALL COSTS END THE SECRET SPACE PROGRAM. THE SURVIVAL OF HUMANITY   DEPENDS ON YOU GRANDFATHER.

MAJOR MATTHEW STEVENS, SECRET SPACE PROGRAM'   :End

Walt worked as an Aeronautical Engineer for Lockheed. In fact, he was their Chief Engineer in charge of developing the company's Propulsion Systems Program. Set up shortly after the end of the war with Germany, Walt had been recruited direct from the Navy with whom he still held a tentative position. In 1944, and after graduating from MIT with a First in Aeronautical Engineering, Walt had enlisted in the US Navy in time to see out the last year of the campaign. Wanting desperately to do his duty Walt never actually saw any combat and was immediately given a commission and posted to a secretive base in the Bavarian mountains to aid research into prototype aircraft that had been part of the NAZI war machine before they had fled the underground complex. Walt had excelled in this field and continued his work after the war with

Lockheed. There was no application process for Walt or any of the other one hundred applicants sat alongside him at Andrews Air Force base in early Autumn 1945. None had actually applied for any of the jobs they would eventually find themselves undertaking. All had been specifically selected for their expertise in their given fields.

The letter had been more of a summons than an invitation to attend. Many of the attendees, including Walt, still wore military uniform. As the panel of speakers addressed the audience Walt didn't immediately recognise them all. He did, however, recognise the man sat in the middle of this panel of five, who waited patiently until the others had completed their addresses before speaking himself. Then, and only then, did the President of the United States, Dwight D Eisenhower, stand and begin to talk.

Walt recalled his short motivational speech. It stuck with him over the years and sprang to mind now as he read the strange message on his television screen. Why he felt there was some sort of connection between the two messages he couldn't say, but thinking back it struck him as having some comparisons. He again recalled Eisenhower's words.

'Gentlemen beware the Military Industrial Complex, of which you are now a part of. There is no going back. This is the future that awaits all humanity.'

Walter recalled that at this point in the President's speech the lights being switched on at the far end of the aircraft hangar, in which they were sat. As the lights illuminated the object at the far end, there were audible gasps from some of the audience. People stood, others pointed, some even clapped. It was then that Colonel Walter Stevens realised that all the rumours were in fact correct.

The Roswell incident was true, the crafts existed, and one of them was situated in this hangar, just meters away. Floating a few feet above the ground.

The last thing Walt remembers from that first day is the president's final words, 'Welcome to the Secret Space Program'.

Walt kept looking at the television screen and the message that was displayed. Messaging systems were developing all the time and Walt was aware of many developments within the industry using a form of instant messaging but for the general public, even the military, it was not yet in existence.

The Secret Space Program was itself in it's infancy and Walt, as an integral part of the programs development, was aware of most of the current technological development programs. This was not one of them.

Walt whispered to himself, 'Who is Major Matthew Stevens?, and why was he referring to him as grandfather?'. He thought about his own son, only three years old and asleep upstairs. Significantly, his name was Matthew Stevens. 'Was this significant?'. He knew this particular three year old did not put this on the screen.

Opening his desk drawer Walt took out a pencil and a single sheet of writing paper. Sitting in front of the television Walt copied the message as it read on the screen. Putting the paper back into his drawer Walt decided another record, more evidential in nature, was needed. Grabbing his camera from the shelf above the desk he proceeded to take several photographs of the television screen. Satisfied he had all he needed he turned off the television. He stood for several seconds then switched it back on. The message was no longer there. It had disappeared.

Placing the camera into his work briefcase Walter called to his wife before closing the front door, 'Back Friday Brenda'. There was only a muffled response, as usual. Closing the front door quietly Walt drove the thirtyfive miles to the airport, parked up his recently purchased Chevy motor car, and boarded a private charter jet along with sixty other passengers. Ninety minutes later Walt, along with the other workers, alighted the aircraft in the hot Nevada desert.

Four silver coloured shuttle buses were waiting to take the workers a further eight miles into the stifling heat of the desert to a complex, part underground, part over ground, and could accommodate a workforce of three thousand at any one time. Given the nickname of 'The Dream Factory', by those that worked there, the official name for this highly secretive compound on all Majestic Twelve documents was Area 51.

Chapter 2

State Corrections Facility, Texas.

Present day

Matt Stevens stared in silence at the ceiling above him. White, everything white. The walls, the floor, the ceiling, white, sterile.

Stevens had resigned himself to the inevitable, days, weeks, even months ago. He had considered his actions time and time again. He had reasoned that if the same conditions applied, he would take exactly the same action. His only comfort was that in taking one life he had in fact saved countless others. Thinking back now to that February morning back in 1991, Operation Desert Storm was in full swing. The Iraq war was quickly finished thanks in a large part to the superior aerial superiority of the Coalition Forces. When Major Matt Stevens took off on the final sortie of the day in his FA-18 Hornet, twin engine multi-combat fighter, he had a bad feeling. His wing man that evening was an Air Force Captain whom Stevens had previously had a run in with over his gung ho attitude towards civilian casualties. His motto was, 'If you've got em, then drop em', referring to any unused ordnance that the aircraft may bring home to base. The day's target, a mobile supply line on the approach to Basra did not appear and the intel was not good. Stevens, as the senior officer, called an abort and return to base. After a four hour flight from Northern Cyprus, Captain John 'Wayne' Calder, call sign 'Cowboy', called in an alternative target sighted. The target was a civilian convoy. Local citizens, with cars, donkeys even, and trucks full of household wares. As 'Cowboy' called in the alternative strike to ground control mistaking the farm trucks for combat vehicles Stevens, call sign 'Quarterback', interrupted.

'Cowboy, this is Quarterback. Negative on the new target. This is not a military convoy, repeat Not Military'.

Cowboy either did not hear or mis heard and brought the second Hornet around in a wide arc until the civilians were in his line of sight. During the first pass Cowboy dropped two cluster bombs which took out at least three farm trucks and a dozen civilians. His cannon fire accounted for at least another six to eight. As Cowboy returned for a second pass Stevens saw the head vehicle, a white van displaying the distinctive red cross. This was not just a civilian convoy, this was a medical convoy.

'Cowboy, this is Quarterback. Desist your attack. This is a medical convoy. Repeat, desist. This is an order'.

Cowboy continued towards his second run at the convoy. As he came within range two sidewinder missiles were released by Cowboy. Stevens could not accept the US Military taking out unarmed civilian medical casualties.

Stevens was coming at Cowboy head on. Flicking the switch Stevens pressed and released his own sidewinder before arcing off to the right and heading back to the Northern Cypriot base.

His last communication of the campaign was, 'Bird down. This is Quarterback. Cowboy is down, repeat Cowboy is down'.

Now, he was about to be taken down.

There were others inside the room, but he paid them no attention. There were people staring at him too, but he chose not to stare back.

There was a clock. It ticked. It ticked so loudly he could feel the passage of time. He wondered whether it was designed that way to remind the occupant of this room of the value of time. He could see the clock. It was a digital clock. How could it tick. He didn't know. He didn't care. Did others think like him or was it just him. He looked at the clock and it read 23.59.

Suddenly Stevens was elevated from a horizontal position to a vertical one. He could now see his audience clearly. Suits, lots of suits, some in Army fatigues too. It was a strange feeling. He seemed to be on display, like in a shop window. Although this was no shop window. There were no smiling faces today at the shop.

Then a voice sounded. 'Do you have anything to say before sentence is carried out'.

Stevens, even at this late stage was defiant.

'I am Captain Matthew Stevens of the Army Air Corps and I regret nothing'.

The suited man who had spoken simply nodded his head and Stevens was brought back down to the horizontal. No more faces, just white, everything white. And three tubes.

His arms, ankles, upper and lower torso were all restrained by heavy duty leather straps. They were heavy, polished but not uncomfortable. They had definitely had some previous use. Stevens knew it, sensed it.

Stevens turned his head slightly to the left, just enough to see his left arm. He watched as the coloured liquid rushed out of the machine up the first of three tubes heading into his vein. He wondered one last time how it had come to this. He was Army and flying mad from an early age and when the opportunity arose to combine both he grabbed it with both hands. He was a Pilot in the Army. He had seen action in both Iraq wars, with medals to prove it. He had only ever carried out his orders. Only one time did he stray, and for the right reasons too. Civilians would have died, many, many civilians. He had done the right thing. Now they were executing him for it.

He could feel the change in his body now, a relaxed feeling, almost pleasurable. The first tube was now pouring into his arm and the second had already set off on its short journey. It was a traffic light system. Why was that?, he thought. A strange thought for his last.

The green had arrived and done it's job. The amber was nearly there. Drowsy now, Stevens fought against closing his eyes. Were they really going to kill him?.

The answer was yes. This was his last battle on this earth and he was going to fight hard to the end. Forcing his heavy eyes open one more time he saw the second tube, the amber one had reached his veins and the third was now heading towards him. The red poison was coming for him.

Struggling for breath now Stevens felt like his lungs were burning. A strange sort of cold burning. Was there an icy wind in here?. His lungs were full of cold air. They were in fact collapsing in on him.

Breathing more heavily, he was panting. He tried to focus on the tubes. It was them against him. How long could he hold out. He fought hard not to close his eyes, and straining now he tried to focus on the tubes again, on the red liquid. It was nearly at the entry point. The battle almost over, he could do no more. The fight was done for Major Matt Stevens as he closed his eyes for the last time.

The warden made a note of the time. It was 00.09. It had taken 9 minutes for this execution, two more than is normal. He would need to report this.

Fifteen minutes later Stevens body was taken from the execution chamber. It was put straight into cold storage.

An hour after that it was collected from the prison mortuary and flown to an Army medical facility in Nevada. Stevens had no surviving family and had signed away his body to medical science years earlier on joining the Corps.

It now belonged to the Army.

Chapter 3

Washington DC

Present Day

Lizzie walked into the room feeling powerful. She was, after all, newly promoted to this position and now had real power. She could do good things.

Dressed in a sharp Stella Mccartney suit she looked the all American girl made good. Lizzie Whitehouse was ready for anything, if not a little apprehensive at not being able to make the planned briefing this morning. It wasn't her fault but nonetheless she would have liked to be more prepared for her first meeting as chair of the Executive Appropriations Committee. The woman entrusted with briefing her had apparently had some sort of road traffic accident. These things were sent to test us she thought. Must send flowers.

She lifted a small Dictaphone out of her purse and voiced, 'Send flowers'.

She'd never been to this part of downtown DC before so when challenging her driver why the meeting was not at the White House, or its associated buildings he simply shrugged his shoulders, 'Just following orders ma'am'. Lizzie reminded him that he was her designated driver and hers were the orders he followed. The driver never did respond to this and so Lizzie sat back and made a mental note to request a new driver as soon as she got back to her own office.

The driver pulled up in front of one of the older office blocks on the West Side of downtown DC. Opening the door for Lizzie he said, 'Ma'am I am advised to inform you that as this is your first visit here you are to take the lift to the basement. The meeting is in the basement office, doors directly in front of the lift'.

Lizzie never responded but simply walked up the steps to the glass doors which were opened for her by a man in a suit, a government man. He simply held out his arm pointing to the lift opposite. She walked over with her back to both the government man and the driver outside. She somehow knew both were staring and watching. She never turned.

Pressing the call button on the lift the doors opened immediately. Walking in she turned around as the doors closed behind her. Sure enough, the government man was stood at ease, hands held together in front of him staring at her. There was no emotion on his face. However, it did feel to Lizzie like he was there to ensure no one uninvited came in and no one would leave unless authorised to do so. Another mental note made.

The doors closed with a gentle click. Looking at the panel to the right of the lift doors there was only one button. It read 'B'. Why no other floors thought Lizzie. Unusual. She looked all around the inside of the lift and sure enough there was only one button. She pressed it. What else could she do. She was going to look into this for sure, later. The doors suddenly opened and another government man was waiting for her. He looked pretty much like the other one upstairs, dark suit, short cropped brown hair, military stance, muscular, serious look. Christ perhaps this is the same man from upstairs she thought, or his twin. He also had his arm raised and directed her towards the door. This door had no handle. The man touched a small metallic square to the right with his thumb. Lizzie waited whilst the man firmly pressed his thumb against the pad and stood straight. She expected the door to open but it took a few seconds. She looked sideways at the government man and saw that he was actually looking into a small glass panel whilst his thumb appeared attached to the other one twelve inches directly below it. His retina was being checked. A loud bleep suddenly brought Lizzie back to the here and now. The door slid open and the government man beckoned her to enter. He did not speak.

Walking into the room Lizzie was taken aback by how many faces there were. Not only that, they were all looking back at her. She could only see one female in the room, that was her first observation. They were all sat round one very long rectangular table. There were no identifying name tags, which she found surprising, just company names in front of each representative. She carefully studied each person briefly and only recognised one person. This wasn't in itself surprising as with any political system there are layer upon layer of representatives and then their representatives, particularly when it comes to allocating funding as she expected to be doing here. What was surprising, however, was the person in the room she did in fact recognise. She had seen his picture many times on TV and his name mentioned often. He had been on numerous red carpet events and was a very well known. The most well known of Hollywood film producers. His name escaped her at the moment, but it would come to her shortly. It was odd that his company tag said 'NASA Public Relations'.

Had she walked into the wrong office?. Perhaps she should be at the 'White House' after all and not some underground bunker in a salubrious part of DC.

Her second observation, and one that only seemed to reinforce her concern that this was not where she should be, was the fact that she seemed to be the only politician there.

She was still stood and as she pondered this last thought, the only other female in the room walked over and switched on the microphone at her desk.

'Miss Whitehouse, welcome. Please take your seat as chair. We are about to start with a presentation from the Northrop-Grumman team. They will outline their latest developments since the last meeting and their required expenditure going forward'

'I was expecting.....'

'I know this is all strange to you but it will become clear after the presentation. Everyone here will give you an up to date position before you sign'

'Sign what?'

'The requisition payments'

At that the young woman returned to her seat, pressed a button and everything changed for Lizzie.

There were some strange clicking noises as if the whole room was being locked down. Then a large screen appeared in the middle of the table. It was not physical, but it was there, sort of holographic Lizzie thought.

The meeting began.

Lizzy Whitehouse was a forty something New Yorker. Streetwise, strong willed, sexy, but sometimes a sucker for good cause. A crusader perhaps.

Recently elected to the Senate she was widely tipped to go far, maybe even the top job itself one day. A Whitehouse in the actual White House. Wouldn't that be something she would often say to herself. She was now there to some degree, but the top job would be something, just for the name itself.

Having studied Law at Columbia she graduated second in her class. Not because the top student was better but more down to her own stubbornness and her, 'I'll do it my way attitude'. Her love of politics also didn't help, often taking her focus away from her law studies and concentrating them on some lost humanitarian cause or political demonstration somewhere. Second place was fine. 'First is worst, seconds best', she often reminded herself.

During her first pro bono year after graduating she chose a small downtown law firm as opposed to the multi million dollar outfits she had been courted by. Again, this avenue was down to her long held political views rather than any materialistic goals. Her democratic socialist views took her to the Bronx and a two partner firm, 'Wendel Associates'. With staff totalling less than a dozen she saw first hand how difficult it was for everyday New Yorkers to achieve the American Dream. Her client base came to Wendel because they offered low rates, free services, no win no fee cases. The vast majority of cases were paid for by the state. Wendel was last chance saloon for most of its clients.

Lizzie was a firm believer in justice for all, not just the few. Everyone had a right to a legal defence whatever your position in society. As it turned out Wendel's clients were, on the whole low down in the proverbial food chain. Clients who could not shop on Fifth Avenue or have a view of Central Park from their balcony. Most were more likely to be seen running from such establishments, being chased by security or police.

They were, however, also victims. Victims who had no chance of retribution against the state or multi nationals should they be victimised in some way. Lizzie represented some of the City's most vulnerable criminals. No hopers, given the most basic of defences that the law could summon up. Often too little too late. Guilty verdicts were the norm but in Lizzies eyes even to get a fair sentence for someone who had resorted to crime because of the bad hand society had dealt them was an achievement.

'Time to fit the crime', was her moto.

In her first six months of pro bono work Lizzie witnessed three executions, lost all bar three of seventy five cases assigned to her, and realised that there is no system at all in the USA that employed fair justice for all. Different sentencing in different states for the exact same crime. Juror selection to ensure guilty or not guilty verdicts. Longer sentences for people of ethnicity. These were all issues she could not accept and vowed to change one day.

Lizzie looked at the agenda on the tablet in front of her. She was still getting used the holographs but looking at the agenda caused her to question the reality she was engrossed in at the moment.

Was this meeting real or was it a dream?.

As agendas went it was pretty standard starting with a list of attendee companies. There was a couple of apologies from some California tech companies along with Facebook.

There was the usual agreement to sign off the previous minutes and a signature she instantly recognised as her predecessor. Senator Watkins from Wisconsin.

She saw representatives from the Aerospace Industry, the Military, Academia, Stanford, MIT, and Cal Tech. There were pharmaceutical companies, NASA, and surprisingly, the media. The CIA were there but not the FBI?.

She made a mental note to find out what the hell the media were doing in such a high level meeting. She would later find out to her horror.

She was the only politician on the list. Wasn't this supposed to be a Public Appropriations Committee meeting?.

Lizzie was deep in thought and had not been paying too much attention to the first speaker when she heard mention of the Moon. This brought her back into focus. The hologram was now showing a 3D image of what she recognised as the moon. The speaker, a man at the far end whom she could hardly see was talking about some construction project on the moon. Lizzie thought she must be hearing something clearly incorrect and was about to speak up when a hand lightly touched her shoulder. She turned to see a man smiling back at her. He was elderly, probably in his 60's somewhere, grey hair but plenty of it. He had an athletic looking build for his age too. There was something recognisable about him, again, as if she had seen him somewhere before. He spoke in a whisper close to her ear.

'Don't worry Miss Whitehouse you'll get used to us'

Smiling back Lizzie replied, 'I'm sure I will but......'

She was cut off by an automated voice that sounded from all around the room.

'Two minutes to broadcast'. 'Headsets on please'

Lizzie was a little troubled. The smiling man still had his hand resting on her shoulder. He was leaning in again.

'Miss Whitehouse, how many of these meetings have you attended previously? It's normal for any new chair to accompany the outgoing chairperson prior to them taking over. How many?'

'None, this is my first'

'Where is your predecessor. He should be here for your first meeting with the NK13 team?'

'He died,.....suddenly'

'You've read the pre meeting briefing pack?'

Lizzie shook her head slowly.

The smiling man removed his hand but leaned in again.

'OK. Then put your headphones on, don't speak. You won't be expected to. Just be ready to sign the papers when presented to you, ok. It's important you don't say anything'.

Whispering back, annoyed now, 'But I'm the chair of the meeting'

'That's your title but you can do nothing. You are the governments representative that's all. Do you understand? I'm telling you this for your own good. The government run the country. These organisations here run the planet'

Lizzie, irritated now questioned, 'I have to be somewhere in an hour. How long will this take?'

'It can take hours. You won't be able to leave until the room is unlocked. We are in what's called Lockdown. No one in, no one out. Wait until everyone else leaves and we will leave together. Trust me. Just sign and smile'

'Who the hell are you?'. 'What is your name?'

'Edward, Edward Aldrin. You can call me Buzz'

Chapter 4

Washington

Henry Hanna was a second generation German immigrant . He had carved himself out a reputable career as a journalist with the Washington Post. He was a trained Economist and after completing his first degree in Economic History he went on to study for a Masters, majoring in journalism. As the sub editor of the daily business bulletin at the Post he lived a comfortable life. Single, he lived alone. A gay man, he did not look to advertise the fact. He took his pleasures where he could, usually for payment, and spent most of his time these days indulging his passion for Astronomy. He had always been fascinated by the stars. It was in his blood. His late father had a low level job at NASA but had been struck down at an early age by a form of Parkinson's disease. Left unable to communicate properly he had been looked after by his mother for twenty years until she died ten years ago, worn out. His father had then been put into care until his death a few weeks ago.

It had come as a relief when it happened. As much as he wished he could have had conversations, a relationship even, with his father, it was useless. He did not show any signs of knowing who Henry was. At the end it was a relief for them both.

Henry was beginning to get something of a reputation in amateur astronomy circles. He spent hours watching, recording, and analysing Earth's nearest neighbour, The Moon. It was his passion, his real love. Economics reporting paid the bills, the stars were an escape for him.

His most recent observations had resulted in some noticeable changes in and around the Sea of Tranquility on the moon's surface. His initial thoughts were that he was observing natural shadowing but when his observations continued to show some marked changes, he began to share these findings on line. If these changes were indeed confirmed, then it appeared that the structure of the moon was changing. How could this be. He didn't know. Either way with his new digital telescope he had acquired he would continue to watch, record, and share his findings.

For now, the telescope could wait. He had to collect what was left of his father's documents from his solicitor this afternoon. Since his recent death Mr Hanna senior had left specific instructions about his burial, property, and belongings. As far as the burial was concerned his wishes were met and he was indeed interred with his late wife at the local cemetery.

His property had long since been sold to cover the costs of his care and the only thing left was to collect the last of the remaining items specified in the will and any sparse monies left over.

As it turned out, after covering all the costs of care, funeral expenses and the solicitors cut Hanna was astonished to find that he was presented with an outstanding amount of $837 to pay. This was the shortfall after all Mr Hanna senior's assets had been liquidated.

The solicitor though, Mr Cohen, did have a package to hand over to Hanna. It had been with the company Cohen &Cohen since Mr Hanna senior had arrived in Chicago some 40 years ago. Henry took the package and left Mr Cohen with a cheque for $837 before leaving for the office. He had a late shift to work, preparing a report on the recent gaps in the government's public accounts. He would have a look at the package when he got back from the office. For now, he had to number crunch.

Later that night Hanna left the offices of the Washington Post feeling a little jaded with a head full of figures. Picking up his briefcase he headed out to a local bar frequented by persons who wanted a quiet end to the day. He took a booth and a waitress came over straight away, 'What can I get ya?'

'Bud, and whisky chaser'

'Coming up'

After the beer and whisky had arrived Hanna took a long pull on the beer before reaching into his briefcase and retrieving the package from Mr Cohen's office.

The package was a typical brown manila envelope that had been sealed many years ago. The seal had clearly been broken before and further seals put in place. In total there were five seals on the envelope. Maybe his father had changed the contents a number of times?. Who knows. Breaking the seal one last time Hanna reached in and retrieved an envelope. Again, it was brown. It was however instantly recognisable and stamped 'Berlin 8 Ocktober1944'.

The swastika stamp shook Hanna. He took the whisky and drank it down in one. Henry Hanna was well aware of his grandfather's history. A member of the German army, and the SS no less. He opened the envelope and took out a letter addressed to his father and a picture. It was history in his hands. He should be glad to hold something of his family's history but somehow this was not the moment he hoped it would be.

The letter was a very brief note to his father identifying his grandfather, his position within the SS, and a pleading to use the enclosed information wisely.

The picture was of a place in the snow, Antarctica was Hanna's guess. His father had told him stories of his grandfather's adventures in the snowy wilderness. There were three men in the picture, his grandfather clearly identifiable even with his fur lined clothing. There was the outline of some distant mountain range in the background, but the fuzzy background made it unclear.

On the back of the photograph were numbers, a set of coordinates. There was also something else in the distance behind the three men. Hanna could not believe what he was seeing. Was this a joke, a long standing family joke? Surely this was a mistake, some photographic trick. The silver looking object in the distance was clearly hovering above the mountain range.

His grandfather was pictured during the war in what looked like Antarctica with a Flying Saucer in the freezing sky!

Chapter 5

Slowly awakening all Stevens could see was darkness. His eyes took a long time to adjust. At first, they refused all his brains instructions and remained closed. His mind was open, but his eyes were still closed, refusing to open and obey his command. Reluctantly they did open and confirmed the darkness all around him.

Was this what death really was? Just total darkness. Eternal darkness?. If so, then he really must be in hell.

There were others here, present somewhere. He could sense it. As Stevens physical senses returned his eyes opened and he became more accustomed to his surroundings. It was however still dark, black even. He was sat down, comfortable. Certainly, more comfortable than being strapped down. He was sat in a seat, in a dark environment. A previous experience flashed through his mind. Was he now sat in a cinema?. There were rows and rows of seats all around him. Others were present, he could see them now. All sat. But this seat was different, not like any cinema seat he had ever experienced. It was so comfortable it was almost as if his body was moulded to it. His mind once again retrieved a past memory from his brain. This time he was flying. Flying a fighter aircraft for the Army. He was a pilot with the Army Air Corps, or at least he was.

Was this an aircraft. Was he being transported somewhere or was this some transitional dreamlike state as he transgressed from life to death. So many questions.

His eyes were now almost fully adjusted to the dark and his bodily senses all coming back on line. He could see that all the seats around him were occupied. There were so many. They kept going and going. So far, he could not see where they ended. He must surely be on a massive aircraft. Perhaps everything he recalled in his past life had been a dream. A nightmare. He hoped so. He was Matt Stevens, a decorated war veteran. An Army Major. A Fighter Pilot.

Sitting back, he began to relax. Closing his eyes again he began to pull his recent memories back to the front of his brain to analyse them. Where had he been before sleep took him. He remembered the wires, the sanitary room, the coloured liquid pouring into his veins, burning his veins. Shaking his head, not wanting to accept the memory recall Stevens reached up to touch his face but he could not. He could not move his hands. His feet and legs too would not move. He was restrained still, as he had been before, not for any precautionary or safety reason but to prevent movement. Stevens began to doubt everything. This was just not happening. There was some sudden feeling of motion. Opening his eyes again this aircraft was actually moving. He had enough flying experience under his belt to know when he was in a vehicle that was airborne.

Looking around the seat to his immediate left was occupied. Female occupant, young, thirty something, athletic looking, asleep. In fact, she looked completely out of it, unconscious even. Maybe dead. All the other seats were occupied, occupied by men and women all in the 25-35 age group he guessed. To his right was the aircraft window. The blind was down. No daylight coming through so this must be a night flight. Stevens did not like to be restrained, and so struggled to free his wrists from the straps. They would not budge. A strange material, they looked metallic and to be a part of the chair itself as if they had been welded to the chair in some seamless way after he had been put there. Stevens could not understand this. His mind was now screaming, 'Release these fucking straps'. All of a sudden there was a click and the straps seem to blend into the seat again. Stevens could now raise his hands. 'How the fuck did that happen. Coincidence or what?'. He automatically rubbed his hands together. They tingled a little as the blood circulation began to return into parts briefly starved. The same with his arms. Stevens briskly rubbed them as if stood on the front porch on a winter morning. The seat had arms, but he could not see the housing for the wrist restraints. He rubbed his hand along the upper, lower and underside but could find nothing. It was as if it was seamless. Stevens could not see or feel any switch that would release the torso restraining strap or the ones keeping his feet in place. All he had at the moment was upper body freedom. Turning toward the female to his left he attempted to reach out to her but try as he might he was a good twelve inches short of making physical contact with her. Same with the seat directly in front. Turning his attention towards the window Stevens felt an urge to lift the blind. If he could he was going to look at the view outside. Stretching his right arm, he was still a little short. Stretching, keep stretching, his body now hurting as the torso restraint gripped him tightly. It was as if the seat was trying to stop him get to the window. Stevens sat back, panting, ribs hurting. He was going to give it one more go. There was a button clearly visible on the bottom edge of the window. He nearly managed it last time. Looks like a standard push and release. Here goes. Stevens inhaled and lunged at the window. Reaching out with his right arm he somehow stretched his upper body like never before and with the edge of his fingernail caught the release button. It was not a push button at all but the momentary contact of his finger with the button was enough. The window blind was instantly not there anymore. It was now clear glass. His ribs hurt. For a moment he had to catch his breath.

Stevens stared. Just stared, unable to comprehend what he was seeing.

Stars, hundreds and hundreds of stars, in a clear black sky. It was so clear. Then another object came into view and Stevens almost passed out again. He was looking at a beautiful image. Something he had seen before but only in books, magazines, and on the television. He couldn't believe it.

He was looking at planet Earth.

Chapter 6

Washington

The lights dimmed and Lizzie put on her headphones. She could hear a count down, spoken in English....'Forty six, forty five, forty four'. Obviously, she had less than a minute. Looking at the list of discussion points on the screen in front of her she quickly scanned over them. Wide eyed she could not believe what she was reading. Surely this was some sort of a prank.

Looking around the room she counted thirty individuals plus herself with headphones on. There were a number of other suited men stood, some in military uniform, plus a couple in odd styles of clothing. Most were stood behind those that were sat at the table, something Lizzie found a little unsettling. There was a man in military uniform behind her chair. Military and secret service minders no doubt, DIA, CIA, could be any number of the alphabet agencies present. What windows there were when she entered were now covered and the room was in semi darkness. The countdown continued,....'Fifteen, fourteen, thirteen'.

One last scan of the agenda and point six was something just unbelievable. She didn't realise it, but she was shaking her head. Buzz tapped her on the arm and stared into her eyes. He mouthed the words 'STILL PLEASE'. Lizzie knew what he meant and nodded. He smiled back.

'Three, two, one'

'Good morning members. Today's meeting will cover the agenda points in front of you and I anticipate it will last no more than six hours. We will break every two hours. There will, as is usual, only be questions raised if I invite them, otherwise as in previous meetings those with input will continue unquestioned and uninterrupted. This is an informative meeting only and one which confirms funding for the next quarter thanks to our respective governments. We have a new chair from the US government today who I trust has been well briefed and will sign the requisition papers when prompted. When I conclude the meeting, I expect everyone to leave promptly apart from the NK13 who will remain'

'Now, point one. The Moon'

Chapter 7

Washington

Lizzie looked up and watched the first speaker touch the screen in front of him. As he spoke Lizzie was mesmerised. She was also shocked, stunned, and generally disbelieving in what was being presented here today. He was talking about a base on the far side of the moon for Christ sake. Why we weren't still allowed to go there. Some agreement between President Truman and the original majestic team from the late 50's which was itself negotiated with the current inhabitants of the far side in return for knowledge. Medical knowledge, anti gravity engineering, the boundary layer, the Van Allen belt and how to get through safely, distance reading capability. A lot of this went straight over Lizzie's head but what she did start to understand was that this was no straightforward government finance meeting.

Should she be here listening to this. She wished she weren't.

The speaker coughed and went on.

'The agreement ends once either we develop our own Inter dimensional travel or the Greys start to mine on the near side of the moon. Both of which are fast approaching. We may need a disclosure strategy, real or false, or, and this is a more favourable option, a second moon landing. A fake one of course but one which leaves some long term base there which we could use to explain astronomical sightings that will inevitably be seen from Earth. We are already receiving reports of amateur astronomers observing anomalies'.

Silence, then another voice spoke. It was the same person who had earlier made the introductions.

'For those of you who are new or forget, there will always be a two minute silence following a members statement to allow the statement to be transmitted to all its destinations, inside and outside of this arena'.

The introducer continued. 'We have decided to make another film in the short term. This should give us at least another ten or twenty years. Mr Scott please, point two'.

After another two minutes had passed Lizzie turned her attention to the next speaker, which she vaguely recognised. In fact, it confirmed her original thoughts when she walked in. It was the Hollywood film maker Ridley Scott. 'What on Earth can he be contributing'.

When he spoke, it became obvious what he had to contribute.

'Members thank you once again for inviting me. I am honoured. In anticipation of this moment I have previously put in place a team working on a second moon landing film. Fictional of course as was the case with the first, but one which I will use as a template for the new broadcast. What I am about to show you is a first draft, a trailer if you like, but a small snippet of what will eventually be man's next small step and broadcast to the people of this planet as we successfully land with Apollo 18'.

Lizzie didn't realise it, but she was staring. Staring hard at Mr Scott. Again, she thought she was in a dream. In fact, she was actually biting down so hard as she stared that her lip bled. This brought her focus back to the meeting as she reached and took a tissue from her pocket to wipe the bleeding lip.

'We faked the moon landing', 'Incredible, fucking incredible' she whispered to herself.

'Whose idea was that?' she said a little too loud.

Ridley Scott turned to her and directly answered, 'Kennedy'.

'Great, so it's true we can fool all the people all the time'

'Actually, he was right about that. Why do you think he said it. He was back peddling and couldn't go through with all the false reasoning'

'So how come we ....'.

'We shot him'.

Chapter 8

Stevens was secured in his seat. This was real. He was not dead but was this was much worse.

After managing to look through the window of this strange vessel a small electric shock brought him back into his seat. Almost like being pulled back, magnetic like, he was sat rigid, eyes front, arms resting, bent at the elbows. He was unable to move them. Indeed, he could not now move his arms, legs, or head. He could just focus his eyes, in front. Perhaps he was being punished.

A screen lit up. Located on the back of the seat in front it was very much in the style of a business class aircraft seat. Stevens head began to spin. He was dizzy, lightheaded, then a voice sounded.

'This feeling will last a few short seconds only'

'Keep looking at the screen in front of you. Do not be afraid'.

There were a few groans from other seats nearby, a couple of screams in the distance. In front he thought but Stevens could not be sure. They stopped abruptly.

He noticed an intravenous line went into his left arm. He could also feel something cold attached to each side of his head. It was as if two cold coins were attached, one to each temple. There were no wires, but something told Stevens they were for communication.

The screen in front became brighter and a digital clock started. It was a countdown. He had less than sixty seconds before something else began. The voice again. It came from somewhere, but he couldn't place the source. It was however giving him instructions.

'Welcome all to The Secret Space Program'

'Your lives have been saved by NK13. You are all now a part of the secret space program. You are a privileged few. You will play your part in saving Humanity as we look to explore the stars. This is your future. You have no other. Embrace it'.

'Watch the screen in front of you as we all take the long journey towards the gate. These are your instructions'.

Stevens realised the voice was coming from inside his own head. The discs were vIbrating.

The clock on the screen read nine, eight, seven......three, two, one.

The screen changed. A map. A map of the solar system appeared. Planets were displayed and the Earth could clearly be seen. The moon also. The moon had a number attached, 2. Earth was 1. Looking more closely Stevens saw the other planets in the solar system, our own solar system. There appeared to be a line, not a line a trajectory from the moon towards the planet Saturn, then on to Jupiter. Jupiter was 3. The trajectory then circled Jupiter a number of times before heading off towards something in between Jupiter and Neptune. It was number 4.

'Fuck' thought Stevens, a 'Black hole'.

As he looked more closely the screen changed showing him a larger scale. It was showing him other galaxies. There was a number 5 on the screen. It was a long way from our planet. From our solar system even. It appeared to be another black hole in the constellation of Vega. Looking closer Stevens could see numbers 6,7,8,9,10,11. There were hundreds of numbers with lines emanating from number 5. This was a road map he now realised. Stevens was headed for the stars. To Vega.

Chapter 9

Washington

Henry Hanna was aware of his family's history. Their German ancestry. He knew he was a second generation German immigrant, whose family had fled Nazi Germany.   He knew his grandfather was in the German army. He accepted that the majority of soldiers on both sides were simply following orders. What he found most difficult to accept over the years was that his grandfather, the grandfather he never knew, was an SS officer.

The Washington Post archives were extensive. Hanna logged on the Post's archive database and began searching. It took less than twenty minutes to discover his grandfather's work history at the University of Hamburg. A First Class degree in Ancient Languages, followed by a Masters in Symbology and Cuneiform script.

Hanna struggled to make the connection. How had that taken him to the SS and the Nazi party?. He was a scholar not a soldier.

There were numerous links to Oswald Hanna, even some old photographic links. There were early photos of his university days, then, after 1938, the smart gentlemen's suits gave way to the German Army Uniform.

Hanna went through the war archives and again found some interesting photographic links with rank and date records attached. There appeared to be some links to a number of expeditions which his grandfather was involved in and a number of group photos taken in locations Henry didn't at first recognise or indeed understand their importance. As Henry flicked through some of the photos one such group photo caught his eye. His grandfather was sat with two other men on the back of an Armoured truck. They were dressed in Army fatigues but had fur lined coats on. All three looked tired and exhausted and all were smoking cigarettes gazing skyward. The interesting thing here was the background. It was all white, nothing but white. Snow and ice everywhere. So white, untouched, virgin. It was actually difficult to distinguish between sky and land on the photograph. Henry gazed at the photo for some time trying to figure out where exactly in the world his grandfather had had this photograph taken. The photo was a microfiche copy of a photograph. It was stamped on the bottom left. Henry couldn't make it out straight away. Hitting the small magnifying glass icon at the top a plus and minus symbol came into view. Henry moved the cursor over the plus and enlarged the photo. Positioning the cursor over the bottom left to centralise the image of the enlarged date he now read.

'1943, Antarctica. Hanna, Himmler, Prost'

After a couple of minutes gazing at the photograph on the screen Henry took an envelope from his briefcase and placed it down in front of him. Carefully opening the envelope, he removed a note on what appeared to be very old and discoloured paper.

'To my son. This war is lost but one day we may have to fight a much stronger enemy. The Reich have sent a message and now someone is coming. In fact, they have been travelling for millennia. It's been 12,000 years since their last visit, but they will soon be here. They are coming home. The Gods are returning'.

'Take care and God bless you my son'.

The note was handwritten. It was from his grandfather to his father.

On the back of the note there was some numbers which Henry recognised as latitude and longitude again. Alongside the numeric series was written in capitals, 'CITY UNDER THE ICE'.

Chapter 10

Stevens watched the screen as it ticked down....three, two, one, zero.

Then nothing. An anti-climax. He felt nothing.

Then, the voice returned as the screen filled up with page after page of instructions. They were in Spanish, French, Chinese, other languages he didn't recognise, each for a few seconds until moving on.

The voice returned.

'Your journey has begun. You may not feel any movement but be advised we are moving faster than you have ever travelled before. Do not be afraid. You will not feel afraid. We will help you adjust.'

'You can now move your arms. When you see your mother tongue on the screen in front reach out and touch it. Then wait. Further instructions will appear'.

Stevens looked around him at row after row of people. He noticed they all wore the same one piece suit, a dull grey colour. Some heads in front appeared to be moving, others were still. No doubt, all were as bewildered as he was.

He was positioned so that he could neither see, touch, or in any way interact with anyone else.

He could move his arms now as instructed. He ran his hands over his face as much to ensure he could actually feel it was him. He wanted some reassurance that this was not still some dream state he was in. He felt something on his temples, discs, one each side of his head. He tried to remove them but a sharp sudden pain in his head stopped him. Head spinning now it took a while for Stevens to regain some composure. He decided to leave the discs alone, at least for the time being. Running his hands over his upper body he could find no pockets, zippers, or any type of fastening. Something akin to Lycra. The garment was clearly an all in one, not his favoured option. Very thin it was warm and cool at the same time, strange. As he moved to his torso, he could feel some kind of belt restraint holding him in his seat. The seat was a good fit too, moulded to his body. It was a perfect fit and as he changed position so did the feel of the seat.

As his hands moved further down, he suddenly felt a slight panic. His groin was hard. Again, a moulded box covered his most important bodily bits. He wondered about taking a piss, panicking again but almost immediately felt relaxed and relieved.

The voice returned. This was definitely inside his head. Stevens felt sure it was connected to the discs.

'Read your instructions. All will become clear'.

Stevens looked up at the screen. The screen read.

'Welcome to the Program. Touch the screen to begin'.

Chapter 11

Stevens reached out and touched the screen as instructed. What the hell, now is not the time for a bad attitude, or a headache. Just go with it.

At first nothing. Then the screen illuminated.

'Welcome, chosen one. We are retrieving your records Major Matt Stevens.

'Fuck sake' thought Stevens. This is like calling cable TV and being put on hold.

It felt like hours but in reality, it was just two minutes of waiting, then another on screen prompt appeared.

'Welcome Major Matthew Stevens to the Secret Space Program. Please be advised that any incorrect response at this stage will result in you being terminated from the programme'.

Then, a number of questions followed, all relating to Stevens birth, parents, education, and military service. At the end of each statement it read Y or N?.

Stevens touched the Y at every point until the screen prompt read.

'Thank you, Major Stevens. Welcome to the programme'.

The voice returned.

'The screen will now show you a short film. Do not be alarmed. This is the true history of the planet you know as Earth. It will also outline to you the history of the programme you have agreed to join, its origins, its reasonings, and its end goal. At the end of the film you will be given further instructions and a set of tasks to perform. These tasks will test your physical and mental strength, your IQ, speed, agility, initiative and endeavour.'

Stevens was mesmerised.

The screen changed, he watched in awe. Could this be real?. Was this true?.

The voice in his head answered him.

'Yes, it is'.

Chapter 12

Henry Hanna spent two days researching the landscape of Antarctica, the variety of research projects, both current and historic, that were recorded along with their co-ordinates.

Over the past fifty years or so there had been in the region of sixty temporary, and twenty five permanent research bases housed in Antarctica. Most of the Western developed world have had cause to put some form of base there at some time. Hanna meticulously plotted the coordinates of every known research facility he could find information on, onto a large scale map of the continent.

Finally, he plotted the co-ordinates written on the back of his grandfather's note to his own dad.

Looking at the map he knew then there had to be some truth in what his German grandfather had said. Some extraordinary event may well be about to re occur and it was definitely connected to Antarctica. Looking at the map again he noted the spread of red pins he had placed on the map. They were spread all over the vast continent, but a pattern did shine out at him. The black pin marked his grandfather's expedition and this one did indeed stand out. There were no red pins within at least five hundred miles of the black pin, the German expedition. Looking closely at the map was like looking at a white circle with a black pin in the middle. All the other red pins were spread in such a way as to form a circle around the black one. It was as if there was a five hundred mile no go area around the German coordinates.

Hanna picked up the phone and dialled.

After being put through to four separate individuals he eventually had someone identify themselves as part of the imaging department of NASA. Hanna had used them before to obtain quality photos of the moon, one of his actual hobbies he was passionate about. It was usually expensive but generally of good quality. It didn't normally take this long to get through though. Perhaps it was because it was the Antarctic. The voice on the other end went through some routine questions about the reasons for the request, the expense of obtaining satellite imagery but eventually got around to asking for the co-ordinates.

Hanna gave the coordinates. He waited then unusually was told, 'Please hold'.

After a couple more minutes the person returned only to advise Henry, 'Just transferring you'.

Henry was kept on hold for several more minutes and was just about to hang up in frustration and call a senior colleague to see if that would help when a different voice came on the line. This voice was different. Efficient. To the point questions were again asked in what Hanna could only explain was almost military in style. After what seemed like an age of repeating the same questions and answers the voice on the end of the phone abruptly stated, 'There are no photographs relating to these coordinates' before the line went dead. The receiver had terminated the call. Hanna sat back dumbfounded. That had never happened before.

Three Hundred miles away in a sterile building deep in the American desert, another person was looking at the same coordinates given by Hanna.

These coordinates did exist, and they were indeed in a remote part of the Antarctic.

Lifting the telephone handset, the man sat looking at the photos on the screen marked 'TOP SECRET SSP ONLY', pushed one of the buttons on the phones base. A voice answered almost immediately.

'Cleansing and waste disposal'

The caller wore a military style uniform but there was something different about it. He proceeded to download a recorded conversation that had been flagged up at the NASA Imaging department with a caller from the Washington area.

The caller gave a Hanna's name and a Washington address.

'Deep clean and dispose'.

'The address, yes and it's occupant, name is Henry Hanna, a journalist apparently'.

Chapter 13

Lizzie was struggling with some of the terminology used by a number of the speakers but the general outline of what was being said was complete fiction, it must be. She was not taking in everything as she was trying to rationalise the main concept here. OK so we are not alone in the universe, nothing too outrageous about that. Most rational people of mediocre intelligence would accept that but......bases on the moon?. Alien bases on the moon, and we're not allowed to go there. You've got to be kidding me.

The speaker was now talking about mineral wealth.

'The mineral wealth on the moon is apparently very much in demand by at least two alien races who appear to have a joint deal to excavate and mine there'.

Lizzie didn't realise but she was shaking her head and whispering aloud her thoughts as the speaker continued to relate that both these alien races have an agreement in place not to excavate beyond the dark side of the moon providing we don't ever go up there.

'We never went to the moon?' Lizzie whispered turning to the man sat next to her. This man, to her left, she now recognised and remembered one of the most iconic, if not short, speeches of all time. He shook his head back at her, 'Keep listening, you'll understand. We did go there but we were not allowed to land. Listen'.

Over the next three hours Lizzie was astounded by what she heard. Some things she learned she had always suspected, like the Roswell cover up and the true account of the Alien crashes. The formation of the CIA, Majestic 12, the fore runner to this current contingent that she herself was now a part of it appeared. Apparently at every meeting she learned there is always a brief history recounted before bringing in any new information on current developments. She wasn't sure why, as she was the only new member. She was also amazed at how much involvement the media had in the cover up. How could they be controlled so easily by such a small group.

She already knew the answer. The media were powerful, but think 13 group were the one's who really made the decisions.

The speaker now changed. This would be interesting as it was someone she definitely recognised from the world of movies. She and the others were being reminded of the contribution the movie industry had made both in the initial cover up and since the late 1950's in the drip, drip, of disclosure. The disclosure of the truth through sci fi films, TV shows and a variety of written publications. The truth was very much out there, it always had been apparently. After initially ridiculing anyone who dared to believe in the Alien question the public believed what was being put out en masse. Farcical accounts and productions that were in themselves satirical and meant to bring to the masses that Aliens were just for the imagination. However, with the onset of modern day investigative journalism primarily having a core of investigators who not only could, but were actively seeking to put the truth out there in a way that would be believed rather than ridiculed. It became apparent that the media and movie industry needed to be on board. The public needed preparing for the truth. TV began to make films and shows that not only had some elements of truth in them but were in some cases basically true accounts.

Accounts of the following films were given and Lizzie was astonished. As a Sci Fi fan she often wondered how things would be if some of the Sci Fi releases ever came true. And now, her favourite Sci Fi movies of all time are all based on truth, 'What, you are kidding me!. Star Trek is real', turning to Aldrin. Aldrin simply shook his head and re directed her to Ridley Scott's proposal. Lizzie never heard anything else he said. She kept repeating the films in her head that were based on truth. 'Star Trek, Contact, Close Encounters, Blade Runner, Alien, ET, Interstellar, Fuck me!'.

Chapter 14

Hanna took the call shortly before 8 am. Breakfast was the one meal of the day he like to enjoy in peace without any interruption from work. The fact that he was getting called so early was unusual in itself. His landline was known to only a few people.

Hanna took the call against his better judgement.

The caller did not identify himself but made it clear he knew who he was talking to.

'Henry Hanna?'

'Who is this?. How did...'

'Is this Henry Hanna. I have something you want, believe me'

The caller spoke with an accent Hanna couldn't place. He wanted to meet, and soon. That morning would be good. The caller stated he had information about Hanna's family, his German family. A location was given to Hanna, 'Ed's diner, downtown Washington at 9am'. 'Antarctica, you want to know what's there then meet me in the diner. I know who you are and what your grandfather found in Antarctica'.

The caller rang off abruptly. Hanna held the phone to his ear not moving. Did he hear that last word correctly, 'Antarctica?'. How could anyone know of his interest in Antarctica.

Hanna knew the place, a regular haunt for local press and media folk.

There had been plenty of calls in the past about his family and its links to the NAZI's, this was nothing new. He had never hidden this away but no one, not even he until recently, had known anything about his grandfather's expeditions. Certainly not to Antarctica.

Hanna replaced the receiver then picked it up again and dialled to try and retrieve the callers number knowing this would be fruitless.

It was, 'Caller ID not known' was the response. He picked up his car keys and left the house.

As Hanna pulled off his driveway in his Ford Galaxy two men watched from across the street. They were casually dressed in jeans and polo shirts. One had a jacket on, the other wore a baseball cap and T shirt. A keen observer would have seen them arrive on the street in a black sedan motor car with two other men. The casually dressed men had alighted the car from the rear seats and had been walking up and down the street for the past forty five minutes. Both wore ear pieces and were taking instructions from the other two men sat in the front of the black sedan, now located somewhere else in the city.

Two minutes after Hanna's departure a white postal van pulled up opposite his house. The two casually dressed men walked towards the van. As they neared the rear doors opened and one by one they were swallowed up by the vehicle. The post van left the suburban street before most of its professional inhabitants had finished their breakfasts and left for work. No one noticed anything out of the ordinary.

Ed's Diner was not too busy when Hanna walked in. Making his way towards the bar he noticed that most of the tables were empty whereas the stools at the bar were largely occupied.

Taking a look around he couldn't see anyone obviously making their way towards him, so he took a stool at the end of the bar facing the door and ordered a coffee.

'Make that two'

Turning Hanna saw that the voice belonged to a black man, late 30's, short cropped hair, moustache, and sunglasses. His hand was held out towards Henry, 'Carter, James Carter. But call me Jimmy'

Hanna was surprised as he looked this man up and down. He didn't sound like the voice who had called earlier.

'I called you earlier, thanks for coming'

Hanna again tried to process this voice with the one he had taken earlier. Maybe it was the lack of caffeine.

The man wore a charcoal grey suit. Not too cheap, not too expensive. A work suit. Everything about this man said military, cop, or government man.

'Shall we?'

Carter didn't wait for an answer as he took both coffees from the bar and started walking towards an unoccupied table. Hanna was momentarily left at the bar but followed the black man to the waiting table. As he caught up with him, the man held up a glass jar, 'Sugar'. Hanna was staring down at the man, now seated. Something caught his eye, something silver, in the man's suit kerchief pocket. Hanna didn't know why but it bothered him. He registered this fact and moved on responding to his question.

'Yes......I mean no thank you. I take saccharin'. Hanna took a small dispenser from his top pocket and popped one into his cup. He took a spoon and stirred.

Looking this man in the eye, albeit through his sunglasses which had remained on, he asked,

'who are you?, what do you want?'

'I told you, James Carter, Jimmy'

'Yes but.....'

'I have information that needs to go public. You can do that'.

'What information?. You mentioned Antarctica, why?'

'That's right. Look, I know about your grandfather. He was a Nazi. I also know he went to Antarctica. More importantly Mr Hanna, I actually know what he found there and where he found it. Do you know any of this?'

Silence.

'I thought not. Question is Mr Hanna, do you want to know what he found there, why the German high command were so keen to go there'.

Hanna took a sip of his coffee then spoke.

'So, Jimmy. Tell me what my grandfather, what my Nazi grandfather as you so kindly called him, found there in Antarctica'

Carter took a sip from his cup. He was obviously enjoying this position of power and was going to stretch it out as long as he could. At least that's what it looked like to Henry, who was now getting mildly irritated.

Hanna stood from his seat and was about to say something to Carter.

Sensing Hanna was getting frustrated Carter interjected, 'Aliens. He found Aliens'

Carter took a photograph from his jackets inside pocket. Hanna was staring back at him whilst trying to digest what he had just said. Placing the photograph on the table in front of Hanna it was immediately grasped by Hanna who stared at it with some intensity. He flipped it over and read the date and coordinates. Retrieving his own notebook, he flicked through a few pages until he came to the notes he had made from his grandfather's letter.

The co-ordinates matched.

Looking again at the picture he saw a vast wilderness of snow and ice. It was a satellite image and in the north western corner a clear image could be seen amongst the snow and ice.

Sitting back in his chair Hanna whispered to himself.

'So, it is true'. Looking up at Carter he asked, 'Can I keep this?'

'Sure'

Carter went on leaning into Hanna's personal space which Henry found uncomfortable.

'I have something else, but I can't hand it over in plain sight. Follow me into the bathroom in a couple of minutes after paying the check'

He had no time to respond as Carter had already risen from his seat and was walking toward the door marked 'Guys'.

Hanna watched Carter move through the door. He made a last glance behind him as he entered but did not look Hanna's way. It was more of a sweep of the whole place.

Investigative journalists often work on instinct and Hanna, whilst intrigued by the photograph, had a bad feeling. He left a ten dollar note on the table and rose from his chair. Walking over towards the bathroom he paused at the door, stopped momentarily, then turned and left the diner leaving Carter waiting. He quickly made his way to his car, started the engine, and drove straight home.

A young couple were sat in the diner, but at the bar. They also left without finishing their meal that morning. As they left the diner, they watched the journalist get into the blue Ford Galaxy and leave the parking area. The pretty young female was not now giggling and staring into the eyes of her boyfriend as she was in the diner. She now had a rather more serious face. Taking a mobile out of her jeans pocket she dialled then spoke briefly.

'He's headed west. Get the blue team to go directly to his address. He's probably heading there, at least some time today. But be quick, he may be on route'.

Agent RS15 is a spray developed by the US Army as an emergency anaesthetic for use in the field of war operations. In the theatre of war. Once inhaled by the recipient not only does it anaesthetise the patient with immediate effect, it also incapacitates them into an almost comatose state to stop them struggling. In the field of war, it gave the Army medics in Iraq and Afghanistan the ability to treat a badly injured soldier. It increased their chances of survival tenfold. Many soldiers are lost as they writhe about in agony following contact. As they thrash about the blood pumps even faster and with it their chances of survival diminish. It was also only a temporary anaesthetic and had a short lifespan. It wore off within 60 seconds and within a few minutes all traces of the compound were gone from the body's pathology.

In effect it was untraceable in the blood after a very short time period, as Henry Hanna would find out to his cost.

Hanna had put his foot down in an effort to get home. He made a quick call to a contact within the local astrological community but after a near miss with a garbage truck going in the opposite direction decided to cut the call short promising a call back later.

Pulling onto his drive Hanna failed to notice there were more vehicles than usual parked along this quiet suburban road. Carrying his briefcase, mobile phone, which was now ringing, and the photograph, he struggled to get the keys in the door lock. Sticking again he reminded himself once again that he needed someone to take a look at it. Eventually opening the front door, he almost fell into the house. He dropped his keys and phone as he stumbled in, then kicked the door shut behind him .

Bending down to pick up the keys he was surprised to see a pair of legs at the bottom of the stairs. They were resting on his bottom stair. Slowly rising he saw they belonged to a young man. Mid 20's, long blonde hair, surfer style, baseball cap, spectacles, wearing a denim jacket and jeans.

Henry Hanna was confused and scared at the same time. This was not normal. The young man held a length of rope.

Trying to be brave he questioned.

'Who are you?. What do you want?'

There was movement to his left. Hanna did not have time to make eye contact with the second male. All his brain would register was a short hissing sound and a cold spray on the side of his face and mouth. The result was instant. That was what was great about Agent RS15. It was so useful. So versatile.

The second intruder, if anyone had been watching, would have been described as the one wearing the gas mask, caught Hanna before he toppled and gently dragged him towards the second male at the bottom of the stairs. The blonde male, now also wearing a gas mask himself, tied the length of rope over the hand rail at the top of the stairs. Lifting Hanna under his arms both men dragged him half way up the stairs before the blonde man placed a noose around his neck. Satisfied that the noose was firmly tightened the blond man gave Hanna one last firm push in the back and he toppled over the side stair rail. The rope went taught and Henry Hanna slowly choked to death.

There would be headlines relating to his death in the local, and some national newspapers in the coming days. The Police would investigate, find some unsavoury pictures of children on his laptop found open in his study and conclude that he took his own life. The case would be closed within a week. His death marked down as self inflicted, no third party involvement.

Chapter 15

Stevens awoke again. He had been put to sleep after the first set of tests had been completed.

This time he was not restrained. At least he didn't think so. Looking around he saw that some of the seats were now empty, unoccupied.

Feeling a little disorientated he had not realised he had been put to sleep until he woke up.

So, he can be put to sleep at any time, as and when, by whoever was running this ship.

'What the Fuck was going on?', Stevens mumbled to himself.

Moving a little the seat felt different somehow. It looked the same but somehow different too. Thinking back to the tests, at least they appeared to be tests, the screen in front showed some basic mathematic formula. He was not actually asked to do anything, but he definitely recognised the mathematics on the screen. As each screen display changed it felt as if he was interacting with it somehow. His mind and the screen seemed to be communicating. The mathematics became more complex with each screen change. Sometimes there was a DNA molecule on the screen in front of him which he recognised. As he continued solving the mathematical equations being presented to him on the screen the equations themselves appeared to be telling him something. Not a story as such, more of a historical account. Stevens realised that with each mathematical formula he was being taken on a journey. The human journey, its origins, and its destination.

Planetary star systems were displayed. Their relative positions in relation to our own Galaxy and each other were displayed. Stevens could see how the Earth was connected to the other star systems. There were some names he recognised, others he did not. Small dots were highlighted on various screens. When he focussed on them mathematical formulae appeared. His mind was asking questions and the computer was giving him the answers. Distances from Earth were displayed mathematically and in a format he did not understand. Some of the black dots appeared to be moving position on the star charts. They were connected to each other somehow.

'No this can't be. How could we know this?'

The dots were known 'Black Holes'. At times the screen went from two to three dimensional. It was like a giant swiss cheese. The black holes were connected to each other in some way. Like tunnels linking one piece of the cheese to another. It hit Stevens then. What he was looking at was an Interstellar map. Focussing on the Milky Way, our own solar system, the screen showed Planet Earth, its moon, and all our near neighbours.

There was what appeared to be an orbit, no not an orbit, a course set around the Earth then heading out towards the outer reaches of our solar system and off into a distant Galaxy.

A numeric number within a rectangular box was flashing. It's current position appeared to be between Earth and the planet Mars. When he focussed on this particular Icon he knew, he just knew, it referred to his current position. The position of the ship he was on.

'Fuck, your joking'. He had a momentary panic but as his body sensed the increased blood pressure and raised breathing rate a reverse action immediately kicked in from somewhere.

There were other boxes on the screen too, hundreds of them. Can they all be vessels. Something told him they were. They were not all flashing, but some were. Some were still within our own solar system, others appeared to be in other star systems. 'Jesus', he whispered, 'is that even possible?'. Again, there was some sort of acceptance in his head and again he knew that it must be correct. The boxes on the screen represented Spaceships. Some of them were billions of miles away. As Stevens selected individual icons an amount of information was displayed on the bottom of the screen.

DISTANCE FROM EARTH

SPACE TIME

LIGHT SPEED

DESTINATION

RESPONCE TIME

'Why were some of the icons flashing whilst others were still?'

That was the last thing Stevens could recall before waking up a few moments ago.

As he now looked around, he could tell that he was definitely in another part of the ship, if indeed you could call it a ship. He was no longer in darkness. The place was illuminated. He could see others sat in seats all around him. As far as he could tell about one third of the seats were unoccupied. The seats that were occupied had both men and women, black, white, oriental in origin. All were aged 20-40 years old he guessed. All wore the same outfit as he was, a steel grey all in one, tight fitting. It reminded him of an episode of 'Star Trek'. The clothing was very similar.

He was not restrained anymore. However, he could not get up either. He didn't understand why. Try as he might his body was not obeying his brain's request to stand.

People were now approaching from behind. As they walked past in single file Stevens saw they were aligning themselves to some of the other passengers. All were dressed as Stevens was, all in one coveralls, tightly fitting. These were white in colour, not a steel grey. There were no markings other than a number on each sleeve and some sort of planetary motif on the left breast.

A woman stood next to Stevens. She placed a hand lightly on his shoulder.

'Stand up!'

The command was not voiced but still Stevens heard it clearly and knew it was directed at him.

Stevens stood and started walking. He was following the woman in white. Others were also following. He was heading somewhere, they all were. He hoped he had passed the test.

Chapter 16

Lizzie had been sat stunned for more than three hours. The man, Buzz, had been nodding towards her on occasion as if to say, 'Yes it's true, believe it'.

But still she could not, at least not all of it surely. It was incredible, too incredible.

A tray of food had been placed in front of everyone and the holographic projection turned off. The lights in the room came on and everyone seemed to relax as if this was just a normal, run of the mill policy meeting!.

Buzz leaned in and whispered, 'The food's good, you should eat'.

'I'm not hungry. I'm digesting this whole incredible scenario'.

'Well digest it fast. Eat some food, mingle, introduce yourself and try and fit in. It's in your own interests'.

'Is that a threat Mr Aldrin?'

'Listen to me. One day at a time. One obstacle at a time. Your first goal is to get out of here, this meeting. You have no power here, trust me'.

Looking Aldrin directly in the eye now, in a defiant stare Lizzie asked, 'Why are you here?'.

Aldrin leaned back on his chair and started to respond, 'Because I.....', before the conversation was interrupted.

'Good afternoon. You must be the new Chair. We're so glad to have you on board'.

Lizzie did not have the faintest idea who was speaking to her, so she forced a smile and responded, 'It's ....great to be here'. The man standing over her took her hand without asking and held it. He was very tall, in fact he was towering over Lizzie which made her feel slightly uncomfortable. He must be in excess of six and a half feet tall. He had a thin wiry body and he wore his hair long, shoulder length. It was white, not grey, not dyed, but an obviously natural white colour. He wore an outfit more suited to the middle east she thought to herself, a long flowing robe type of garment. His most striking feature though was his piercing blue eyes. As he held her hand with his intense stare it felt as if he was looking inside her, reading her thoughts. Lizzie was increasingly uncomfortable, as the man still held her hand, firmly. Whilst she maintained her smile inside her head she was screaming, screaming to be released from his grip. She momentarily closed her eyes and whilst nothing came out of her mouth inside screamed, 'Let my fucking hand go or I'm going to cut all your god damn hair off'.

The release was instant. The man stood upright. He was indeed a giant.

He spoke, 'My apologies. You must eat. It was enlightening, Miss Whitehouse'.

As the giant walked away Lizzie turned back to Buzz and whispered, 'Who the hell is he?'

Buzz had a mouthful and mumbled back, 'A representative from afar. Now eat'.

Lizzie was about to ask what or who he represented but thought better of it. The room was silent, everyone appeared to be eating, in silence. So, she ate her food as told. It was good although she didn't know what some of the delicacies were. Some type of nut, exotic vegetables, water. Basic but surprisingly healthy and nutritious.

Precisely thirty minutes after the tray was placed in front of her, a man appeared from behind, reached in, and took it away. She was still chewing but just about finished so she let it go. Looking up she could see that everyone's food trays were being hastily removed. Some of the delegates began to stand. Others sat. There was movement as some of the delegates wandered over to speak to each other.

Buzz leaned in again, 'Thirty minutes free time. Go introduce yourself and get a feel for these people. The meeting will continue in half an hour. This is half time by the way'.

Chapter 17

Stevens walked past row after row of seats. He followed in line just like any military officer would, without question. There were others in front, maybe 20-25, all walking in unison. He knew there were others behind too, but he didn't turn to check. Not that he wasn't curious, he certainly was, but something was prompting him to keep walking, continue straight ahead.

He calculated that there were ten seats per row, and he had so far walked past fifty rows. He continued walking. He continued counting. Stevens saw that many of the seats were now empty. Some, many in fact, were still occupied. Men and women of all colours and ethnic backgrounds were sat, focused. All wore coveralls like his own and Stevens noticed that all had certain letters emblazoned on the rear of their garments. Some were obvious and it was clear the letters referred to their role or perhaps their previous role. Maybe those still sat were no longer part of the program. He calculated he had walked past seventyfive rows now. Most of those sat had 'GP' in black emblazoned on their backs. Some had 'Medic' in red. A number had the '^' sign in green which Stevens took to mean they were infantry. So, there were medics, Infantry, GP, whatever that was and Pilots for sure on board. One hundred rows now and still walking, that was one thousand seats, and still walking. No verbal communication from anyone or anywhere. Just silence as Stevens marched on, two hundred rows and still no sign of stopping.

After five hundred rows Stevens abruptly stopped. They all stopped. Five hundred rows, five thousand seats, which likely meant that this craft had at least five thousand people on board to begin with. Stevens was a Pilot. He had been on board some large aircraft in the past, piloted some big birds but this leviathan was something else.

Movement again. He was walking now, at a slower pace. He found himself in the middle column but there was no movement either side, only his line was moving. Up ahead was what appeared to be an entrance of some sort. As he walked through, he and the others were confronted by three persons. Two men and a woman, military he assumed. At least they were dressed in a more military style. This was somehow comforting to Stevens. Recognisable, familiar. He lined up along with about twenty others, all facing the three military looking personnel.

The room was empty apart from a large screen behind the trio. The walls were grey in colour, had a plastic looking texture to them, shiny, could even be a type of glass Stevens judged. There were a number of squares clearly marked on the floor. They were randomly spread across the floor of the whole room. Trap doors were Stevens first thought, surely not. A slight rumble and a feeling of movement underfoot brought Stevens attention back to the trio in front. Any feeling of concern was quickly replaced by a relaxed feeling. A voice, the person in the middle of the three addressed them.

'Welcome to the USS Leonidas'

'You have all been hand picked for this momentous journey you are about to take. You will have questions. We will endeavour to answer them to your satisfaction'.

A pause and then the voice continued.

'You have all been given a second chance. A chance to make history. There are no options left for you. Embrace this new journey you have begun. Look at it as a wonderful opportunity to make another giant step in mankind's history. There are no other options for you'.

Another brief pause.

'Welcome to the Secret Space Program'

The room went dark. The walls suddenly changed and went to opaque glass. Outside the scene was spectacular. Stars, bright stars like jewels in the night sky streaming in. Streaming past. There was no sign of Earth anymore. One bright star shone brighter than the others outside. It appeared to be where the ship was headed.

'To answer what you are all thinking. Jupiter. We are headed to the planet Jupiter. But first we have an appointment with Mars '.

Chapter 18

Lizzie was becoming more and more exasperated and, without realising, quite disruptive.

This latest speaker was, or at least purported to be, German. He spoke German which Lizzie had translated via her headphones. He looked German, tall, athletic, blonde hair, blue eyes. He actually wore a military uniform. He was arrogant too and spoke of technological developments that were beginning to rival the 'Tall whites' and other visiting species. They were, however, feeling constrained and would one day like to return to their origins. It was their leaders last dying wish for his descendants to return home, to the place they were forced to leave over seventy years earlier, Germany. The Fuhrer wants to be laid to rest in Germany.

'Are you kidding me?'

Everyone looked towards Lizzie. The tall man, the German if that's what he was, stared at her.

Lizzie stared back.

'Are you telling me...am I hearing this correct. Adolph Hitler made it out of Germany to Antarctica?'

'Are you telling me there is a German fucking colony in Antarctica?'

The German smiled back and spoke directly at Lizzie in accented English.

'Of course there is'

'Well, when I get....'

A tap on her shoulder from her neighbour caused her to stop.

Aldrin interrupted her raising his voice above hers as he did so.

'Miss Whitehouse is new to this environment. She will adapt and become accustomed to the ways of the NK13. Please continue Herr Hamler'

A slight nod of the head and the German continued but Lizzie heard no more. She was seething, at both Aldrin for interrupting her and at that fucking arrogant bastard that looked like he had just walked in out of a concentration camp.

A German colony in the ice fields. How could the USA have allowed that to happen?. How could the World?.

'We helped them'

A voice spoke but it wasn't the German.

Lizzie looked up but the German was still droning on about their latest technological breakthrough in artificial skin and how more willing or unwilling donors, they didn't care which, were required.

Lizzie wondered who had made that last remark. Looking around the room she noticed the tall man with the long white hair. He was staring at her. His piercing blue eyes were boring into her, it was as if she could feel them looking inside her soul.

'It was me'

She heard it. His lips did not move but she definitely heard it in her head. What the fuck was going on here. She wondered what she should do. She stared back.

He was still staring at her.

'Please just listen'

He was still staring.

Lizzie thought and asked the question in her head as she stared back.

'Are you talking to me, inside my head, you with the long white hair?'

He was now nodding at her and Lizzie was scared. Was she just imagining this?. Had she just been given some sort of drug.

'We are your friends. Please remember that. Mr Aldrin, please look at her and smile. She needs some reassurance'. No lips moved.

Lizzie didn't dare turn her head. For a long moment she just stared at the tall white haired man on the opposite side of the room. Slowly, very slowly, she turned towards Aldrin.

Sure enough, there he was facing her with his beaming white smile.

'Fuck'

Chapter 19

Approaching Mars

'You are all dead men'

'You are dead men re-born. Re-born to live again. Embrace your new life and you will flourish. A long extraordinary life is yours to grasp'

'You may never see Earth again, but you will see wonderous things. You will experience unimaginable things. Embrace your time'.

Stevens was stood with six other men. Why was that? He pondered. The woman addressing them was dressed as they were but something different was happening.

She continued in a loud commanding tone.

'We are Team Three for Zeta'

'We are an eight strong team and we are an experiment. Many others have gone before you. None have returned. Signals are still returning from multiple destinations in the Galaxy. Not one has returned. You are unlikely to return'.

Stevens heart rate increased momentarily. He started to sweat. Was this fear. He was not normally afraid of anything, so this sensation was not one he had experienced often. All of a sudden, a coldness rushed into him, his veins, his head, everywhere. His heart rate slowed, and he was back to normal, attentive, composed. This he knew was not normal. He could get his heart rate down through breathing techniques learned in the Army whilst in flight school. This was artificial, he knew.

The voice from the speaker boomed out again and he was once again mesmerised. Not just by the tone of the voice which was itself engrossing and pitched at a level which caught the attention of his brain, but also by the content that was being delivered.

'Your telepathic controls will shortly be de-activated for a period. This may have already happened to some of you. You may feel a sense of panic initially, but this will not last. For the next thirty days you will train, learn new techniques, and prepare for what could be a very long journey. Possibly even your final journey'.

'We currently have two pilots, one security officer, one scientist, one linguist, an Engineer, Doctor, and one Team Captain. I am the Captain'.

There was a nod from the Captain, and it was as if a switch had just been turned off. Turned off inside Stevens head.

Stevens felt himself again. He felt in control. Turning towards the others he watched their reactions. One was touching himself all over as if looking for something he had misplaced.

Two others were stood very still, too still, still in shock maybe. A loud bang to his left brought Stevens attention round to the two guys who were stood behind. One was now lying prone on the floor, collapsed.

The Captain spoke again.

'It will take time to adjust. Any questions'

One voice piped up, 'Yeah. Just one. Who are you?'.

Stevens stood still waiting for an answer. He hoped he had not overstepped the mark.

'I am the Captain. You are the Co Pilot, he is the linguist, he is the First Engineer, him the Scientist. Unfortunately, he, indicating to the man on the floor, was the Pilot'.

'You will all meet the Doctor shortly. She will be responsible for all your physical and mental needs. Also, your general wellbeing'. There was an emphasis on ALL from the Captain which Stevens wondered about.

Someone else spoke, the linguist.

'Why us?'

'You were all dead men. You know this'.

'But I was innocent', protested the linguist, a thirty year old black male, athletic build. Very military.

The Captain spoke again.

'You are all military men here chosen for this mission. I do not know the reasons why you were chosen so cannot and will not discuss this. There will be no turning back. You will train, you will adapt, you will be modified if need be. If you are not up to the task you will be replaced. You will complete the mission'

'What do you mean modify?', the First Engineer questioned.

The captain took hold of the front of her collar and tore the tight fitting garment revealing her naked upper body. There was a long scar running from just below the left collar bone to just above her navel. Another one ran length way down her left arm. What appeared to be a battery pack was protruding from her inside upper left arm.

'I am human......mostly'.

'I have been modified where appropriate. Where there was a problem, it has been fixed'.

'Your psych controls are all switched off at the moment. As long as you remain in control of your emotions they will remain off, at times'.

Pointing to her left. 'Living, eating and medical quarters this way'.

Pointing right. 'Everything else'

'Eat, sleep, purge yourselves for the next twenty four hours. You will return to this room for your next briefing at 0800 tomorrow'.

The captain turned and walked towards the direction of 'Everything else'. A door opened on her approach and she was gone.

There were just seven of them left in the room.

Chapter 20

Lizzie glanced at the papers in front of her.

A man in military uniform had approached and with a 'ma'am' had placed the bundle together with a fountain pen, pot of ink, and a blotter, directly in front of her. The speaker at the front addressed them both.

'Thank you, Captain'.

'Madam, the first of your signatures are now required for the warrants before you'.

Lizzie gave a slight nod of the head in the general direction of the speaker as she started to read.

Lizzie was startled as if something on the papers in front of her had just jumped out at her. 'These are execution warrants' she questioned.

'Yes madam. Two hundred to be precise. The first is scheduled for midnight tonight'

Lizzie felt hot. She was flushed and felt claustrophobic. Surely there was due process to follow. Signing execution warrants was for local state governors.

Almost in a whisper as she went down the list of names she mumbled, 'But I don't......'.

A hand took hold of her shoulder, firmly enough to stop her short. She turned towards the owner of that hand, Aldrin.

Squeezing her shoulder with his right hand he pointed towards where the signature is required with his left.

'Just here madam chairperson, just here please'

'Just two hundred more, or possibly two hundred and one'. Aldrin whispered the last figure so that only she would hear it.

Lizzie looked into his eyes. There was a serious look in them. It was a threat. In that she had no doubt. Would she really be two hundred and one if she refused to sign?

A now all too familiar voice in her head spoke again.

'Do as Mr Aldrin asks Miss Whitehouse. It is in everyone's best interests'

Aldrin was nodding.

Lizzie was shaking inside. She did not look up. Instead she took a few deep breaths, picked up the pen, dipped, then started to sign.

It took the best part of forty minutes to sign and date two hundred execution warrants. Each one was taken from her by the military man stood behind after every signature. As the pile grew smaller Lizzie started to slow down and took to reading the names.

There were names from Washington, Michigan, Texas, Ohio. In fact, there were names from all corners of the USA. She noticed that all were in the age range of twenty to forty years, mainly men, but not all. At least eight women so far and all to be put to death within the next thirty days.

Worryingly for Lizzie, there was no mention of any crimes that had been committed on any of these warrants. Was that normal?

They must be capital crimes so most likely homicides. Lizzie continued to sign. There were so many questions running through her head.

Why so many?

Why so many military personnel. Had they been involved in some sort of war crime?. Some atrocity she was not aware of?. Then the last one, a name she recognised from the past. Could this be right?

Then, as quickly as they appeared, they were taken away by the Captain.

A voice brought her back to the present.

'Thank you, madam chair. We will continue'.

'Why so many military personnel?'. Lizzie had stood without thinking. Everyone else was sat. She looked towards the speaker for an answer.

The speaker looked around the room and as Lizzie followed his stare, she noticed that the majority of those sat were nodding some sort of approval.

The speaker spoke again as if annoyed by the interruption.

'I will answer your question on behalf of the group. Please sit, as I will'

Both the speaker and Lizzie took their seats.

'We, and you, are part of something extraordinary. This planet's resources are finite. They are dwindling away at an ever increasing rate. Planet Earth has been plundered for its resources and it has been going on for millennia, and not just by the human race'.

'It is time we sought an alternative. An alternative resource pool and an alternative place for sanctuary. For human survival which at this time is not, and I repeat this for your information, is not guaranteed.'

'To continue as a species in the cosmos in which we live we need to go in search of alternatives. Think of it as looking for options to move to other neighbourhoods in the future. The difference being that the new neighbourhoods will be inter galactic'.

'To do this we need Pilots. We need Navigators. We need scientists. We need to recruit heavily for the Secret Space Program'.

Lizzie questioned. She could not help herself. 'Secret Space Program?'

'Yes. What we as a group do, is look after the interests of humanity. We are looking to ensure the future survival of all humanity, here on planet Earth, or elsewhere in the Universe. We have been looking for some time now and are just beginning to see some positive search results. The public face of the US space program is NASA. This is a front. It is not the main focus of our efforts to travel in space. For that we have a secret space program. It is much more advanced than the public realises but it does come at both a heavy human, and, financial cost that the public would not understand'.

'But executing….'.

'The warrants you signed today have simply ended their existence on this planet. They may have taken their last breath on Earth, but rest assured they have not taken their last breath. They have been recruited to the Secret Space program. Most will be recruited without any prior knowledge but there are some who volunteer'.

'So, what is the point of killing these people?'

'We are not killing them. We are offering them an alternative to death. They simply go to sleep one day and subsequently awaken to a whole new world. A world in space. They are the new explorers. The difference being that for these explorers there is no going back'.

Lizzie fell silent. She was thinking this through. There was something here that she was not comfortable with. At least not yet anyway.

'Miss Whitehouse. I sense you have reservations about being part of this program?'.

The speaker continued.

'This planet we call Earth is not ours. Yes, we inhabit it and have done for a very long time. We call it home. But others have been here before us and others may well be here long after we are gone. It has many names to many different species this planet we call Earth. Humans have been here a mere blink of an eye. In timescales you can comprehend we have actually been on this planet in our current form as homo sapiens for about 40,000 years. The planet we call Earth has in fact been used by Extra Terrestrials as a research planet for millions of years. There has been wave after wave of evolution here until about 40,000 years ago. At that time, we had a helping hand in our evolution, and from then on, we have been left to evolve on our own. We don't know why, we're not sure by whom, although we have our suspicions. We were left to our own devices for the next 35,000 years or so and since then, particularly in the last 2000 years we know the planet has been re visited by both pro and anti homo sapiens species who have left their mark. In the last 100 years, to ensure we develop our technology and consciousness, the pro homo sapiens, maybe even our own creators, have visited more often. You will be aware of Roswell? Well things have moved very quickly since then'.

'Roswell was real?'

'Of course it was. Have you listened to what I have just told you?'.

Lizzie nodded. 'I understand completely'.

Chapter 21

There were seven of them at the moment. Seven if you were only counting human beings. The other person in the group Stevens wasn't really sure what she was. Supposedly a medic, psychologist, mother figure, physical trainer, confidant even. She was, as she said when she welcomed them all to the recreation room, available to help them with all their physical, mental, even sexual needs.

She was there to get them through the journey in any way she could.

'I am Jill', she announced At least that was what Stevens heard as they all walked into the recreation room.

'Talk to me. I will answer where I can'.

It soon became apparent that Jill was in fact 'GIL'. Genetically Induced Lifeform.

Gil explained that during the journey ahead she would become invaluable to them. She would train them, organise them, and prepare them for what lay ahead. She would also command them. She was the team leader.

Gil explained to them that each day would be compartmentalised. It would be split into four distinct groups. Refreshments, Training, Exercise, and sleeping. All at regular intervals.

'There is no day and no night on this ship. As such your new daily time clock will consist of a twenty hour cycle. You will get used to this and it will help you should we reach our destination which has been calculated to rotate once every 20.02 hours'.

Gil continued after a pause. There were no questions coming from the group, so she continued.

'Each day will start with refreshments for one hour. This will also include personal hygiene. You each have a wrist band attached to your left arm. You cannot remove this. Do not try. This will help you with your routine. It will instruct you where to go and what to do'.

'This will be followed by two hours of physical exercise. You can run, swim, cycle, walk, climb, anything, but you must raise your heart rate to a desired level for a period of time. You will soon adjust. Your wristband will help you'.

Stevens examined the band on his left wrist. It looked like a pretty standard fitness strap. Silver grey in colour, it had a shiny glasslike feel but was also pliable. Turning his wrist over he could not see how it was attached. There appeared to be no clip or fastening device as if it was moulded into place again. He touched it but nothing happened.

'Look at the bracelet. Either ask it a question or just think it and you will get a response. It is linked to everything on this ship, me included'.

'It will respond. It is tuned into you. This is a training period. I will now leave you all to familiarise yourself with your environment'.

With that Gil turned and left the room. Stevens noticed that as she approached a doorway, she tapped the bracelet she wore on her own wrist and the door opened automatically. He looked around him at the others. They were all stood, apart from one man who had taken a seat at a table. He was drinking something. Stevens walked over to the man. He looked up as Stevens approached.

'Coffee', he said nodding to the steaming beaker on the table. 'It's not too bad either. Over there, a machine. You can get anything to drink but no food, or alcohol unfortunately'.

'Too bad, about the alcohol I mean. I sure could do with a drink right now'

'Stevens, by the way, Army Air Corps'. He held his hand out to the man.

The man looked up at Stevens and for a brief moment Matt Stevens thought he was going to ignore his attempt at an introduction. He appeared to be weighing Stevens up as if making an assessment.

'Parker, Navy seal'. They shook hands and Stevens was aware of others behind him.

Another voice from his left side, again hand extended, 'Hayes, Naval Engineer and field medic'.

'Olsen, linguist, Ex CIA'

'Connors, US Marines'

'Brotherton, Royal Air Force, Pilot'

'A Brit responded Parker'

'I'm afraid so, but I did once date a Canadian if that helps'

'It doesn't 'replied Parker.

'Let's get some coffee and talk this through anyways', said Olsen.

'Mine's a tea' said the Brit.

Chapter 22

All sat round the table drinking their chosen beverages.

Stevens spoke first.

'So, we've got two pilots, two soldiers, an engineer, linguist, medic and the erm........the trainer I suppose you'd call her'.

Parker nodded, 'Hmnn. Not much of a team to go where man has boldly not gone before eh'

A recognisable voice came from behind them.

'But a team it is'

All turned at once to see Gil. She was stood at the far end of the room.

'In five minutes, you will all follow me to the training area. You will be undertaking your first training session that will equip you for the long journey ahead'

Almost immediately there was a vibration coming from Stevens wristband. The digital display was flashing 'EXERCISE'. More worrying for Stevens was the feeling that there was a connected feeling in his head. Not a vibration as such but a switch had most definitely been turned on. All six men stood. There was no need to ask they all just knew to stand. They turned and started to walk towards the rear of the room, a room that would become known to them all as the kitchen. They took the middle of three doors which opened up into a long corridor. After speed walking for what seemed like an age but was no more than five minutes in reality Stevens smelled a familiar aroma in the air. It was a smell from his childhood school days and his Army training. It was chlorine.

The door in the distance ahead was a bright blue colour. The whole vessel was very bland in nature. Everything was steel grey apart from the doors which were all primary colours. Blue, Red, Yellow, and Green. There were also alpha numeric symbols on each door which Stevens guessed gave an indication as to their position on the ship. The door he was now approaching was marked L4A6. There were also a series of lines and dots below the alpha numeric symbols. Stevens noted this but thought no more of it as it wasn't any code he had ever seen, but very similar.

Parker, the Navy seal was directly in front of Stevens. Parker stood in front of the blue door and waited. Nothing seemed to be happening. Parker raised his right hand and placed his palm onto a glass plate located to the right of the door at chest height. Parker held it there as the glass illuminated. A thin red line, very much like a laser, rose from the bottom of the glass square and slowly made its way upwards scanning Parker's hand. The door opened and Parker walked through. There was an even stronger smell of chlorine. Then, as suddenly as it had opened the door slid closed again. Stevens did exactly as Parker had done and placed his palm onto the glass square. As with Parker, Stevens palm was scanned, and the doorway opened. Stevens walked through, hit once more by that overwhelming smell of chlorine.

Stevens walked over to where Parker was stood and waited for the others to come through.

As he waited to be joined by the rest of the team Stevens looked towards Parker and saw that he appeared to be transfixed. Following his gaze, he saw what Parker was looking at. A massive swimming pool. Stevens estimated It must have been three football stadium sized pitches in length by two wide. He could just make out that there were buildings both below the water line and above the water line. There were what looked like disc shaped craft under the water connected to dome like structures. It looked like it was fifty meters deep.

It was amazing to look at. Further to his right were a number of other teams of individuals, maybe ten or twelve in total, all stood at the edge of this massive pool.

Some were still clothed in their daily work uniforms, whilst others were naked apart from very brief swim trunks. Strangely, there were no females. Also, all the males appeared to be very similar in build to himself and the others on his team. Six foot tall, give or take, one hundred and seventy pounds to one eighty, muscular, no body hair in sight. All very uniform.

Chapter 23

Lizzie rubbed her shoulder and could feel the small lump just under her skin. She couldn't believe that someone would have the sheer audacity to assault her in this way. She was angry again. Even Aldrin's attempts at reasoning were not working this time.

'All members have this simple procedure. It's for your own good'

'Why?'

Smiling again Aldrin spoke softly.

'Everything you have heard and gone through today is unbelievable. I know it is. I've been through it myself, and I felt exactly the same. And I was an astronaut.'

Aldrin moved in closer to Lizzie, well into her personal space which she didn't like one bit.

'There is a bigger picture and in time you will understand, even embrace the program. It's why you were chosen'

Coughing, Lizzie could barely get her words out, 'Chosen?'

'Yes Lizzie, chosen'. Aldrin let his words sink in before continuing. 'One day you may represent us on a much bigger stage with much more at stake than electoral votes. One day you may be representing Humankind in negotiations, not just the United States'.

They were alone in the room. The last two apparently. Aldrin had stayed after the last of the NK13 had departed.

He was behaving like an adviser, mentor even. Aldrin could see she was processing the events of the day.

He went on, 'Yes I am here to advise you, to help you through these initial phases of your new role. I also think you still need proof'

She nodded, 'Yes I think I do need something else, something tangible, physical even'

'Ok It can be arranged'

Lizzie looked up at Aldrin who was nodding at her.

'Ok Lizzie, what do you want. A trip to the Moon, Mars?. It can be arranged, trust me. I can get you to the Moon tomorrow, Mars may take a few days, possibly by Friday?'

Lizzie smiled for the first time today and took his hand.

'Thank you Buzz for making me smile. There's no need for a trip quite that far, even if you could arrange it'.

She released his hand and openly laughed.

'Shopping on 5th Avenue, New York would be fine'

'Ok, you are on!. Just give me a second. If you want to get all your things together. I'll just make a quick call and we can leave together'

'Sure Buzz'

Lizzie picked up her briefcase, opened it, and started putting all the briefing documents from today's meeting inside. There wasn't much to show for an eight hour marathon meeting but at least she had an agenda with some hand written notes. She had a new Nokia/Lockheed tablet which she would apparently need for any future meetings. It was all she would need apparently. Thinking about it, Lizzie didn't realise that Nokia were in any way linked to or worked with Lockheed, an aerospace company. Still, after today's meeting anything was possible.

Last of all was her new government issue credit card. Running it through her fingers it looked like any other credit card apart from the fact that the only markings on the card were her initials followed by the title of the group she had just met with. Steel grey in colour it had a two-tone sort of sheen to it. When turning it over it seemed to switch from grey to green to purple then back to grey. It was silky smooth, traditional size of card with rounded edges. It was very thin, possibly paper thin and pliable. She was assured that you cannot damage it. It would not break, if bent it will return to its original shape, it would not burn or melt in any way and no implement however sharp could cut through it.

Its only markings were on the bottom left corner. 'L Whitehouse LWNK13'.

She was also told that it would be accepted by any outlet, machine, or bank without question for any amount up to $1,000,000.

'One million dollars. Yeah right'

As Lizzie put the card into her handbag there was a rumble beneath her feet which startled her somewhat. 'Whoa'

It felt like movement. A minor earthquake? She thought. She stood and started walking towards the door which suddenly opened. Aldrin walked in.

'Ready?'

'What was that?'

'You'll see'

'It felt like an earthquake Buzz. What the fuck's going on?'

'It was nothing really. Happens all the time here'. Aldrin had a thick woollen coat on. Strange thought Lizzie.

A loud buzzer sounded, and a green light illuminated above the door in the corner of the room. Lizzie hadn't noticed that particular door before. She was now stood at the door Aldrin had just walked through.

'This way. Hope you've got a coat with you'

'Why would I need a coat?. It's fine in DC'

Aldrin smiled and gently guided her to the door in the corner. He held a card in his hand. It was just like the one she had been given and just placed in her handbag.

Turning towards Lizzie, Aldrin spoke.

'Ready?'

Lizzie just glared back at him, hands on hips as if pleading with him to get on with whatever he was doing and get her out of this place.

Touching the card against a small glass panel there was a beep and the door slid open to reveal another long corridor with doors leading off. It was similar to the one she entered earlier that day but not the same she knew. She thought nothing of it. Clearly, they were leaving through a different exit.

The walk down the corridor was a long one. Longer than the one earlier, considerably longer. And colder, getting more colder as they progressed.

'Is this the back way in Buzz?'

'You could say that. Nearly there'

There were some steps ahead Lizzie noted. It was really cold now and she wrapped her arms around herself as she walked.

Aldrin gestured for Lizzie to climb the steps first. She complied and walked up a total of eight steps onto a small platform. There was a door in front of her. It reminded her of the sort of thing she had seen on television, in submarine films. Yes, that was it. It looked just like one of those hatches, metal, tightly fitting, not letting anything in from the outside. There was no window. It was very smooth, no wheel in the middle to open it. There was however another glass panel to the right at shoulder height.

'Try your card Lizzie. This might be a good time to try it out'

Lizzie did as was suggested. She took her new credit card from her handbag and placed it against the glass panel.

A buzzer sounded yet again, followed by a 'click' and the door slid open.

As the door opened to reveal the outside Lizzie could not believe her eyes.

Chapter 24

It was snowing. Lizzie watched in awe at the sight of snowflakes falling on to virgin snow. She found it hard to comprehend what was in front of her. Was this real?. Had she been given some hallucinogenic drug?.

She tentatively took a couple of steps into the snow. It crunched underfoot. Lizzie shivered, wrapped her arms tightly around her body and continued on into the snow.

She was looking at Central Park, New York. No, she was actually walking in Central Park, New York City for goodness sake. She was looking at Bow Bridge and further on she could clearly see the New York skyline.

Is this another stunt pulled by Aldrin or someone else from that bloody meeting? Lizzie started to shiver uncontrollably. It was cold, real cold, New York cold.

Something was placed on her shoulders. Warmth again, then a voice.

'I knew you'd need this', Aldrin was beside her.

'This is indeed central park, New York. Its where you wanted to go'

Lizzie turned, 'But how....'

'I can't explain it to you Lizzie, not the engineering behind it. All I do know is that we didn't develop it. I can tell you that there are a number of other gates throughout the world, all interconnected somehow. They have been here for millennia. We don't know how they work, we don't know who put them in place but we have our suspicions, but we do know how to make use of them'.

'I,...I don't understand'

'Why would you?. Neither do I. These gates have been put in place a long time before we moved into the neighbourhood. We also suspect that they may link Earth to other locations, interplanetary, interstellar even, but as yet we haven't managed to figure out how to open the gates to any other portals,.....yet'

Lizzie spoke softly, clearly confused. 'Who'.

'The EBENs gave us the technology and the infrastructure to use the gates. We think that they, the EBENs could give us more but like everything there is always a trade off.'

Aldrin went on. 'We didn't build the gates, we don't maintain them, but we do have limited access to use them. You left Washington DC a few minutes ago Lizzie and now you and I are standing in Central Park. We are in New York. Come on, let's go get a coffee'.

Chapter 25

The pool was not just big, It was gigantic.

Stevens and the others all lined up at a point near the point where they had entered. Now wearing one piece swim suits very much like a surfers wet suit but much thinner in texture, they awaited instructions from GIL.

There was equipment nearby. Stevens saw what looked like underwater breathing apparatus, and some sort of underwater propelling system.

The pool itself reminded Stevens of an underwater cavern he had once been to in his youth. Whilst the edges surrounding the pool were tiled like any other swimming pool, the walls above them and below the water surface were not. They were cavernous in look and feel. Stevens had run his hands over the wall as he emerged into the cavern. The walls were rock, or at least felt like a lava rock but coloured a dusty red. Looking up he saw that steps had been moulded into the sides, perhaps cut with some implement to allow access into what appeared to be caves. Some of the caves had figures carved into the wall's above and below. One of the cave entrances was part of a large carving of a snakes head, or at least some sort of reptilian face with the open mouth the entrance. Was this a replica of a place on Earth?. Was it from somewhere else, where they were headed perhaps?. Stevens didn't know yet but was determined to find out. If he was going to be part of this program, and he clearly had no option there, he wanted to know everything he could about it. If he was going to die for it then he wanted to know it all.

Gil walked in sporting her swimsuit .

'Gentlemen, please put on your face masks and flippers as I am doing. We will enter the water and you will all follow my lead. I know you can all scuba dive. Follow me'.

There was a splash and she had entered the cavernous pool. They all followed without question. She sank below the surface and swam down into the dark depths. They all followed.

That was the start and each subsequent day they followed the same pattern. They ate, they trained, they had physical exercise, and they slept.

The first four weeks were intense and followed a very full on routine and rigorous training pattern. Most of the training and exercise blended together. They were being brought up to speed physically and mentally. Stevens, like the others had all gone through military training before and he knew they were being prepared. Each week that passed Stevens noticed that his body was becoming stronger. His muscles were more accentuated, his stamina improving, and his strength improving beyond anything he had experienced before.

There was no real indication of when it was night or day, but Stevens wrist band worked on a twenty hour cycle. Gil had told them that here was a reason for this and that their bodies and mind would adjust after a period. That said the whole environment was set up so that the lights came on when their wrist bands indicated 0500 and duly started to dim down at 1900 precisely. With their regular rest periods during each daily cycle this didn't seem to bother anyone anymore other than the linguist, Olsen, who appeared to be constantly tired.

Tonight, they were all finishing off an unremarkable meal in the kitchen. Their wristbands indicated they had ten minutes left then a further period of training. This was unusual as the norm after their last meal was an hour of free time then sleep.

Stevens drank down the last of his water and watched the others. All seemed to have accepted their situations, better than he had himself he thought. Were they wondering why and where they were heading like he was, questioning everything?. He didn't think so. Was he not as controlled as the others?, a stronger mind perhaps?. He didn't know.

Parker was staring at him, watching him. As Stevens stared back Parker returned to his food and concentrated again on the plate in front of him. Parker spoke without looking up.

'You think too much Stevens'.

As Stevens was about to answer the door opened and in walked Gil.

She stood by the open door and waited. Stevens knew she would remain there until the refreshment period had ended. Looking at his wristband he saw there was ninety seconds remaining. Watching the timer Stevens knew that as soon as the clock hit zero and a new training period began, she would speak. As it hit zero it vibrated and indicated the time was 1800 exactly. Gil spoke.

'Gentlemen, please follow me'.

They all stood and followed Gil, the genetically induced lifeform, through the door. This was not the one she entered from though. In fact, Stevens wasn't sure he had seen this exit before. Passing through the doorway Stevens, who was last in the line of six, sensed something was about to happen. This corridor was very narrow. It had a claustrophobic feel to it. They had little room either side as they walked. It also had a metallic feel to it and there was nothing on the floor. They were now walking on a metal grill, a suspended metal grill. The narrow width of the walkway was very similar to walking through the hull of a submarine. Stevens didn't know why he was surprised as they were in fact on one massive ship, a fucking spaceship. There were overhead lights to illuminate the way every 25 meters or so. They were dimly lit and illuminated just enough to see the route ahead. Touching the walls as he walked Stevens felt as if he were running his fingers along very fine sandpaper. Every ten meters some metal supports broke the journey his fingers were taking. The surface was very cold to the touch, even though the temperature around them was very ambient in nature. Stevens realised that he was running his fingers along what he suspected was the external wall of the ship. The other side of this wall was space. Movement up ahead brought Stevens back to focussing on the current task. A left turn quickly followed by a right turn brought them to a blocked doorway. Gil put her hand against the glass panel and the door opened to reveal an identical corridor that appeared to be exactly like the one they had just walked along.

This time they walked in silence for what seemed like an age, but which was only probably 10 minutes. The wall felt cold to touch still and the lights were lit, but only just enough to light the way. Stevens noticed that there were no markings anywhere now. Nothing to indicate their location on the ship. No warning signs of any nature, nothing.

Abruptly, Gil stopped and turned to face them all. She had her back to a doorway, a hatch. She was holding a pair of sunglasses which Stevens hadn't noticed before and put them on.

'Put on your protective glasses now'

Each member of the team, Stevens included, reached down towards a container near the hatch and took a pair of these eye protectors. Ski glasses thought Stevens. They were all exactly alike, not beach style more ski style which fit snugly on to the face with a raised side piece to ensure no light could get in from the side. They were an airtight fit too and felt to Stevens as if they were now glued on to his face. They were initially cold on the skin, but the feel quickly adjusted to skin temperature. Now Stevens could hardly tell anything was attached to his face.

Gil walked up to each team member and either made a slight adjustment to the side of the glasses or simply tapped the front to ensure a tight connection.

'Prepare yourselves' she instructed as she returned to the front. Gil once again raised her hand to a glass panel and the hatch slid open.

Light flooded the corridor. Sunlight. Stevens followed Gil and the others and was truly amazed.

The room was enormous, a giant goldfish bowl full of amazing light beams. Walkways were spanning the centre and perimeter of this spherical shaped auditorium. Following Gil, they took up a position a few meters away from the entrance. It didn't matter that they only walked a few meters into this cavernous spherical space. They appeared to be the last group to arrive. There were hundreds of others inside along with them. All were facing the same way. All wore the same silver grey coveralls. All stood to attention focussed on what was in front of them, the sight outside of this amazing glass sphere. There were twelve hundred persons inside the sphere all gazing out into space in amazement. The sunlight flooded in and they all continued to marvel at the sight of the giant Red planet in front of them.

They were all looking at the planet Mars.

Gil spoke.

'This is Mars. The fourth planet from the Sun and the second-smallest planet in the Solar System. Referred to as the 'Red Planet', it's colour refers to the effect of the iron oxide prevalent on Mars' surface, which gives it a reddish appearance distinctive among the astronomical bodies visible to the naked eye. Mars does indeed have a thin atmosphere, with surface features reminiscent of the impact craters of the Moon and the valleys, deserts and polar ice caps of Earth. Indeed, Mars was once very similar in development to that of Earth. With it's re-colonization it does have a use but it's days as an advanced civilization are long gone. The days and seasons are comparable to those of Earth, because the rotational period as well as the tilt of the rotational axis relative to the ecliptic plane are similar'.

Stevens knew Mars has been explored by unmanned spacecraft. Mariner 4, launched by NASA in 1964, was the first spacecraft to visit Mars, making its closest approach to the planet on July 15, 1965. In 1976, Viking 1 performed the first successful landing on the Martian surface. Like most aviators with an interest in Space, Stevens looked on in awe as a young boy at the pictures sent back. What Viking 1 actually found on the Martian surface would have been an even greater defining moment for the majority of people on Earth had the Secret Space Program not already had several bases on the Red Planet, and only allowed Viking 1 to transmit back to Earth the very much redacted information it had actually gathered. This was all part of a long standing cover up, very much understood and accepted by the most knowledgeable in the Astro Scientific community. And now by Stevens and his team.

Stevens, like the others stood still, mesmerized. How many other humans in history had ever had the opportunity to stare at the planet Mars, like this?. The ship was clearly now in orbit around the red planet and travelling at around 20,000 miles per hour. Stevens quickly worked this out to be around six miles every second. Travelling at this speed the Martian surface looked like a red desert wasteland as it whipped past below them. It was like looking at a giant red football that had been kicked around in the dust. The planet appeared to be one big swirling dust storm with few breaks in the enormous dust clouds. Stevens tried to focus on the breaks in the storm clouds. His eyes were tired, but he thought he had just seen what looked like structures on the surface. There, again, he started to raise his hand and point towards the surface without realising. Had he just seen what looked like a city down on the surface.

Then, a voice spoke. It was inside his head, probably inside everyone's head.

'This is Mars. Welcome to the Red Planet. Look at the surface of the planet. This is the closest neighbour to Earth, your home planet. It has many secrets and for some of you, your journey is at an end. Your task is to uncover those secrets, learn from them. You will make this your life's objective. You will not leave this planet. You will spend the rest of your lives here. Good luck to you. You have already been selected and your Gil will shortly escort you to the embarkation point and your transportation craft.

Stevens glanced at Parker who was looking in his direction and shaking his head as if to say, 'It's not us'.

Stevens nodded back understanding what Parker meant but wondered how he could know this.

Since waking from his 'death sleep' as all his team had dubbed it, all their training had been geared towards a lengthy piece of space travel, potentially a year or more. The Zeta star system had been mentioned on more than one occasion and this was felt to be their likely destination as far as Stevens and Parker were concerned. For now, his thoughts and focus returned to Mars and the words being spoken in his head.

'Humans have been travelling to Mars for over three decades. This may surprise some of you but not all, particularly those of you with some in depth knowledge of science. Mars was once a thriving planet. An advanced civilisation inhabited the planet millions of years ago. They were not space travellers as far as we can tell. There were oceans at one time and the atmosphere was similar to that of Earth. We do not know why, but Mars atmosphere changed around 20,000 years ago. The planet began to heat up, oceans dried up, vegetation ceased to grow in abundance, and all carbon based life forms began to die. About 12,000 years ago, some of the Martian inhabitants, numerous species, but definitely not all, were rescued and taken to it's nearest neighbour, planet Earth. They were spread over the planet we call Earth, and all began to thrive once again. The main species that was rescued from Mars and brought to Planet Earth was a species we all know as homo-sapiens, humans. Humans originate from this planet, Mars. You are all looking at your home planet. We do not know as yet who brought the human race to Earth but we are trying to find out. As our orbit gets closer to the surface you will see structures that you will recognise. Historical structures from the past, and some modern ones from the present. We are seeking answers to our own history and our future destiny. What happened on Mars could, and most likely will, happen on Earth. Furthermore, we are responding to signals received from all over the known universe. We believe they are invitations and we are responding to them. You....are responding to them. You will observe the badge you wear on your uniform. Your insignia shows two planets in close alignment orbiting the sun. The bright blue number seven occupying the middle of the sun is what you represent. You are the seventh wave'.

Great thought Stevens. What this is in reality is a seventh attempt at contact. What the hell happened to the other six?.

Looking to his left Stevens saw the hundreds of personnel all staring outwards towards the planet's surface, still mesmerised, still upright in steel grey, like steel grey ammunition awaiting to be fired off into the cosmos. Looking more closer to home he saw that his team of six were stood in line with a small gap before the next six. This went on and on and on along the whole perimeter. Like a Naval ship coming into port at the end of a long journey with the crew lining the deck. Only this journey was just beginning.

Stevens looked around for Gil. She was some distance away which he thought was unusual. Then it hit him. Of course, there were many other Gil's just like theirs. They all wore a black coverall, not grey, and were a mixture of males and females. They all looked identical though. All the female Gil's looked like theirs whilst the male Gil's also had a very identical physical appearance. They had made no attempt to change or modify their appearance, one clone fits all, or two it would seem. The females all had a white European look about them whilst the males all had an oriental look.

Stevens wasn't sure whether every team had its own Gil or whether one Gil looked after a number of teams. A quick glance and Stevens estimated there must be about forty Gil's in the room, at least. This meant that each Gil would have to look after four or five teams each which would make some sense. Refreshments, training, exercise, and sleep. The four components of their day. Gil tended to be around at some point during each period, but she seemed to spend most of her time with them whilst they were training.

Stevens pondered, she was running four teams, he was sure of it. Each Gil had four teams. She was supposedly going to be with each team throughout their journey. She had told them this. She would be with them as they passed through the gate.

Stevens suddenly realised with a very verbal response what was going to happen.

'Fuck' he exclaimed just enough for his team to hear.

'What', Parker whispered.

'Look around Parker. There are too many teams and not enough Gil's to go round'

'So', Parker was shrugging his shoulders.

'Well, don't you see. We are still being assessed. There is still some thinning out to do soldier. I reckon we are now down to a one in four chance of being the team that goes through the gate'

'And if we don't. Where does that leave us?'

'Exactly'

Chapter 26

A short walk through Central Park brought Lizzie and Buzz to a small diner, Bellfields. Lizzie had walked in silence the whole way and now sat at a window seat looking out, very thoughtful, very pensive, very dangerous, thought Buzz. Placing two black coffee's down Buzz just waited, allowing Lizzie to take everything in. He wanted her to talk to him, but was prepared to wait. He needed to assess her commitment. It was always the same with a new chair. He liked her. He hoped she could see the bigger picture. And it was a really big picture to take in.

The diner itself had seen better days but had a good reputation for serving good food at a good price. It was three quarters full and the clientele were mostly blue collar, either eating after a hard shift somewhere local or filling up before their clock on time. There were pictures of boxers, past and present on the wall, some in large black and white photographs, some in full colour. All were signed.

The lighting was low which gave the place an atmosphere. It also covered up the fact that the floors could do with sweeping. The smell was a mixture of strong coffee and burning fat. There were two women on the hotplate both engaged in cooking. By the sound and smells coming from their direction they were cooking ham, eggs, and bacon, lots of it.

Lizzie took a spoon and stirred her coffee. There was no milk, cream, or sugar. She just needed to stir and watch. The liquid swirled, very much like the universe she thought.

'What happens now Mr Aldrin?'

'Nothing where your concerned'

'So, let me get this right. I just turn up once in a while, when called upon. I sign the cheques and keep quiet. Keep everything I found out today from the American people. From the voters who put me in office?.'

'Yes'

'But why?. Don't they have a right to know. We're spending a lot of their money on something they haven't agreed to'

'There are a lot more people out there than you think that already know. Even more suspect we have a secret space program. But the vast majority don't know, don't care, and would not want this information interrupting their lives. Most Americans just want to go to work, put food on their table, have a beer and dance at the weekend, then do it all again the following week'

Lizzie looked up and was about to say something, but Buzz continued.

'Look, one day I'm sure there will be full disclosure. But not just yet'

'But why?'

'Survival'

'Survival?', Lizzie appeared concerned turning to look directly at Buzz. A waitress approached with a pot of coffee. Buzz waved her away before she could get too close.

'That's right survival. Didn't you listen to anything that was said today?'

'Well, it was such a shock. I couldn't take it all in. I'm still not sure whether I'm dreaming or not for Christ sake'

'Okay, well this is what you are going to do. Go home, do your job, do some good in the office you've been appointed to, but most of all, keep the fucking secret. Do you understand me Lizzie. It's my job to make sure you keep the secret and sign the fucking cheques'

'If I don't, keep the secret that is'

'We'll find someone who can'

Lizzie stood from her seat.

'Is that a threat Mr Aldrin?. I could have you arrested for that. Put you in prison'

'You could certainly have me arrested but no one would believe your allegations. I would be out of jail in hours and both you and I would be replaced in our respective roles and disposed of'

'You don't have that sort of power'

'I don't, but those I work for do. I no longer have a choice in what I do. What's more, neither do you, trust me'

Still stood, Lizzie was angry. She looked away from Buzz. A waitress, the same one with the coffee pot returned only now she appeared concerned.

'Everything ok ma'am'. Her accent wasn't New York, more New Orleans. Lizzie smiled at her,

'Yes, thank you, I'm fine'.

The waitress looked at Buzz and gave him a stare that was more of a threat than an offer of a refill. Turning her attention back to Lizzie she returned the smile then moved on to the next table.

Buzz sat back against the seat and with a sigh tried again to bring Lizzie on side. He felt he still had a few good years left in him and didn't want them cut short by some idealistic Politician.

'Lizzie, some people have great responsibility thrust upon them. Some individuals have family responsibility, some have only themselves to be responsible for. For some they have some local responsibility from holding some locally held office, a few have National responsibility. You, on the other hand, are one of a select few on this planet that have been chosen to shoulder enormous responsibility. A responsibility that goes beyond the national level. One day, hopefully not in your lifetime, but the day will surely come, when we have to leave this planet.'

Aldrin took a breath as Lizzie sat back down.

'We left Mars once before. One day we may have to leave this planet'

Lifting her head to face Aldrin she now had tears in her eyes. In fact, they were running down her cheeks, her expensive mascara following.

'When a ship sinks Lizzie, it's very rare that everyone on board makes it onto a lifeboat'

Nodding, Lizzie finally understood as Buzz continued.

'We're planning for when this ship sinks, again. The human race must survive Lizzie'

As Lizzie took a tissue from her pocket to wipe her eyes, Aldrin stood. He placed a twenty dollar bill on the table and left without another word.

As she wiped her eyes there was a hand on her shoulder. Lizzie looked up to see the waitress again.

'Don't worry ma'am, I've seen his kind before and all I can say is your better off without him. He's too old for you anyway'

As the waitress collected the cups and the generous payment Lizzie whispered back,

'I think your right but it's too late now. I'm stuck with him'

Chapter 27

Stevens was sat at his small computer console in his living space. This small cube reminded him of his college days, a sort of dormitory but on a grand scale.

Inside his living cube he had a bed, not single sized, but not quite a double either. Somewhere in between. He was currently logged on to the ship's information and training archives regarding the planet Mars. On leaving the observation globe all of the team were instructed to go back to their rooms for further training in private relating to Mars and their specific specialities.

Stevens had been trying to research the planet's history, but the system only gives out information it feels the questioner requires. Stevens wanted to know more about ancient Martian civilisation but could not find out about the atmospheric conditions and how they would impact on flight. He did however manage to recover information relating to orbital velocity and discovered that this vessel would orbit Mars for a total of twelve circumnavigations before being catapulted off towards Jupiter.

Stevens wristband buzzed and indicated it was time for thirty minutes of physical exercise.

'What, you've got to be kidding me'

It was unusual for any exercise to be undertaken this late in the day, and for only thirty minutes.

The cube door slid open and in walked Gil. She looked different somehow. More woman, less trainer somehow. She still wore the one piece suit. The hair was the same, but something was very different. She smelled different, a familiar aroma, one he'd experienced before. 'Crikey, thought Stevens', she was wearing perfume. He liked the smell. She also wore a bright red shade of lipstick, he liked that too. It felt familiar somehow.

It should have felt familiar too. The fragrance was one of his previous girlfriend's favourite. Chanel number 5 was a favourite of women all over planet Earth. Gil knew everything about Major Matt Stevens. She knew he liked his girlfriends to wear Chanel Number 5. She knew he didn't like women who wore a lot of makeup but did have a penchant for bright red lipstick.

Gil also knew he liked women in red underwear to match the lipstick. Gil knew what the whole team liked, and she was set to accommodate them all. In due course. Fortunately, this current team were all keen on Gil's but where necessary a John could be supplied.

 Stevens was the first on the list, but she would go through them all in the next four hours or so even if it meant waking some of them up. Sex was important to both physical and mental health. Gil was there to keep them all safe, and healthy.

Stevens just stood and watched, a little confused. Gil reached behind her and pulled a long zipper down to the middle of her back with her right hand. She then used her left to pull it the rest of the way. As she slowly removed herself from the tight fitting one piece, Stevens for the second time today stood watching in awe at the beautiful sight in front of him. Unable to take his eyes off Gil his jaw dropped even further with the sudden realisation of what was so different about Gil. She was a beautiful woman. She was wearing lipstick, Red lipstick, his favourite. Less than a meter away from him. Stevens felt a little feint as the blood in his veins all rushed southward toward his lower torso. Wearing a red lace bra and matching panties she suddenly appeared in Stevens personal space only inches away. He looked down at her ample cleavage. His erection was overpowering. She took his right hand and placed it on her left breast. Stevens closed his eyes. It felt wonderful, something he had long since given up hope of feeling ever again.

'You like this?'

Nodding, unable to speak properly Stevens gasped, 'Yeah'

'What do you want to do to me?'

Opening his eyes Stevens replied, 'What can I do?'

'Anything you like'

Gil sank to her knees. 'First, let me relieve some pressure'

Gil was an expert and within seconds Stevens was gasping and then groaning as he held the back of her neck. It was over very quickly. Gil pushed her panties down, removed her bra and lay down on Stevens bed.

'Twenty three minutes left'

Stevens smirked and kicked off the rest of his garments.

Chapter 28

After her coffee with Aldrin, Lizzie had come to a decision. At least in the short term.

She would play along with the NK13 group, attend their meetings as required, sign the cheques, and take in as much information as she could soak up whilst conducting her own investigations. Her own father, a Supreme court judge, an uncle in the CIA, although he won't admit it, plus a number of well placed friends in the world of media, academia, and journalism, would allow her to look a little deeper into this group, its origins and its future goals. Ultimately, she herself would decide what to do with the information, not Buzz Aldrin. Not this NK13 group, not even the president. She would decide.

The 'ping' from the microwave oven brought her back to today. The meeting was long gone. Three weeks had now passed and nobody had even asked her why she didn't return to her office for over 48 hours after the meeting!. Leaving the cafe after Aldrin was a good thing. She was glad he left her to her thoughts that day. By the time he had left she had had enough of his company and was about to tell him so. She walked through the New York snow towards Central station stopping off twice on the way.

The first stop was a footwear store where she had purchased a pair of knee length boots, discarding her office sling backs into the nearest trash can. The second stop was a sports wear store where she purchased a very expensive winter coat. She needed a new ski jacket anyway so this was an ideal opportunity to try out her new all purpose card given to her that day by the NK13 group. She very much doubted it would get her anywhere, but she did have her own AmEx card at hand just in case. At the sales desk she asked the cashier to remove the sales ticket and further enquired if this was a contactless payment till.

The cashier nodded glancing up at Lizzie as if to say, 'Isn't everywhere'.

Waiting for the cashier to put the sale through Lizzie turned the card over in her hands. It felt like plastic but also like a lightweight metal. The only markings on it were her name and an embossed coloured circle which on closer inspection she would later realise was the planet Earth. Her name and the planet were on the bottom left corner of the card.

The screen bleeped and the cashier looked up, 'It's ready ma'am'

Hesitating briefly Lizzie checked the amount showing on the screen. $399 dollars. The ski jacket was expensive, but she was assured that anything under one thousand dollars would go through without question. Lizzie touched the screen with the card. It bleeped immediately and showed 'Authorised'.

'Thank you ma'am. Have a nice day'

Lizzie put on the coat and walked slowly through the light falling snow towards Central station.

She caught the overnight sleeper back to Washington arriving into the capitol just after 06.00 am. Instead of going back into the office Lizzie went home, showered, packed an overnight bag, then went in search of the gate Aldrin had taken her to the day before.

Sure enough, just after 11.00 am Washington time Lizzie once again opened the door onto Central Park, NYC.

As Lizzie walked through Central Park for the second time in twenty four hours a plan was coming together in her head. Forty minutes and a cab ride later through a bustling New York City, she found herself stood outside the main entrance of Columbia University's Astrology department.

Back in her university days Lizzie had found herself infatuated by a fellow student. Thinking back now, stood on those imposing front steps of the grand Art Deco entrance to one of the country's top Ivy League learning institutions she took a moment to travel back. Even now she wonders where things would have gone had that relationship developed. The culmination of a friendship turned emotional attachment, turned one night stand, could have led to a more fulfilling permanent relationship had her logical common sense brain not kicked in to overpower her warm fragile heart. A mutual love of running and physical fitness at University soon developed into extra running sessions. Meetings for coffee quickly turned into lunches, long evening meals, and a general feeling of comfort in each others company. Any excuse to be close at hand and tactile with each other soon followed and it was this feeling of closeness that culminated one evening with sexual intimacy. Both had decided on a sleepover and after a few glasses of a very strong Barolo wine, both had changed into their respective nightwear. Both girls had recently split from short term heterosexual relationships, something that at the time Lizzie didn't consider significant but looking back now maybe it had played a part. Anyway a very mischievous Suzanne, her closest friend, whilst gazing out her window at the night time stars, asked Lizzie if she would trust her instincts. Just this one time. Lizzie giggled and said she would as she pulled her loose strap back onto her shoulders. The last time Lizzie had worn this nightwear was the last time she had stayed over at her ex boyfriends, an expensive red silk camisole with matching French knickers. Suzanne too was wearing something not quite appropriate for a friendly sleepover, black lace vest and black lace briefs. Lizzie wondered why she had brought these for a girlie sleepover when she had many more sensible options . As she had walked out of the bedroom to the sofa Suzanne had returned from stargazing at the window and was already waiting for her. Suzanne was holding two more glasses of wine and held one out to Lizzie. Taking the proffered glass Lizzie sat at the opposite end of the sofa and giggled again.

A second bottle of Chablis followed, more giggling, and a lot of strange questions from Susie followed. The girls had both migrated to the mid sofa area and their legs were touching.

They both wore their hair long and had used any excuse to run their fingers through each other's loose hair. As Susie pushed Lizzies hair around her ears her fingers lingered on the back of her neck. Lizzie liked this and closed her eyes. Susie was gentle.

'That's nice', she whispered.

Lizzie giggled. Susie was focussed on Lizzie now, her nipples were hard and her face flushed. She whispered to Lizzie.

'Do you trust me Lizzie?'

'Yes of course' Lizzie responded with another giggle.

'Then keep your eyes closed'

'Why'

'Please Lizzie, keep them closed, for me'

'Okaaay', another giggle.

'Drink your wine down, drain your glass' Susie whispered in Lizzies ear placing the glass in her hand so she could keep her eyes closed. Both girls then drained their glasses.

'Promise me you won't open your eyes Lizzie. I can't do this if you open them'

'Uh, huh. What are you going to do?'

'Just relax. Say stop and I'll stop ok'

Susie took off her lace vest and pants. If Lizzie had been watching at this point, she would have seen her nipples completely erect on her ample breasts.

Moving closer Susie was now only an inch away from Lizzie. She whispered, 'I'm very close now. Can you feel how close we are?'

'I can, yes'. Lizzie had stopped giggling and her breathing had changed. It was like a bolt of electricity. She could feel her heart pounding but didn't know why. Susie put her arms around Lizzie's waist and drew her in close. Lizzie did not resist.

'Do not say anything', Susie whispered, holding Lizzie close. 'Just hold me. Eyes closed'.

Lizzie did as she was instructed. She held Susie, held her close. She knew Susie was naked. She didn't mind. In fact, she liked it. After what seemed like an age but was only seconds Susie started to gently caress Lizzies lower back placing her hand under her camisole. Lizzie felt an electric thrill and gasped, 'Uh, hmn,,,'. Lizzie held on to Susie even tighter. Susie's gentle touch was thrilling. Lizzie responded by massaging Susie's upper and lower back. Susie was now gasping and could not hold back. She placed her right hand on to Lizzies left breast. This wasn't a first for Susie although she suspected it was for Lizzie. Susie knew exactly what to do. Lizzie began to pant. Lizzie's camisole was now around her waist and Susie was taking her other nipple into her mouth, using her tongue like Lizzie had never experienced before. Lizzie took hold of the back of Susie's head and pulled her in closer, harder. Lizzie was wet, very wet and without prompting, opened her eyes, lifted Susie up from her breast and kissed her. Gently at first, then with complete passion.

Exploring each other, orgasms came to both, firstly on the sofa, then in the bedroom. It was a wonderful coming together of two kindred spirits.

That was the last time Lizzie had seen Susie. Until today, she hoped. She had called ahead and, after some initial shock it soon became apparent that they could still be friends. A meeting was arranged and here Lizzie was.

Walking back into her office was like taking a step back in time. Both embraced tentatively.

Lizzie spoke first.

'It's been a while Susie, or should I say Professor'

'Yep, Professor Walsh it is. Still gazing out at the stars. And look at you, Senator Whitehouse'

Laughing Lizzie responded, 'Yeah, that's me, still trying to save the world'

After some more small talk that revealed that Susie was in fact now divorced, had a child at University, and was in a long term relationship, with a man, another academic, Lizzie revealed that she had had a number of failed relationships but had never married. Still single and looking for the perfect partner.

'They don't exist Lizzie, believe me. You have to make the best out of what you can, trust me I've tried all sorts'. Susie blushed and there was a slightly uncomfortable delay in conversation as both met each others gaze for a brief moment. It ended when Susie turned and sat at her desk, all business like. She was in fact trying to regain some composure feeling a little unnerved in Lizzies presence.

'So, Lizzie, what can I do for you today?', blushing again.

This raised a smile with Lizzie, and she made sure that Susie could see that she too remembered their last meeting together even if neither was prepared to discuss it.

'Well.......what can you tell me about the constellation of Lyra and Zeta Reticuli'

'Why Lizzie, have you suddenly discovered the stars?'

'Something like that. Also, what do you know about the planets in those star systems. Anything would help'

Susie was staring at Lizzie, 'Interesting'

'Why?'

'Why, because on the astrological section of the world wide web, those two locations have repeatedly had the most hits since the 1980's. And what's even more interesting is that most of the hits are recorded against official agencies, government backed, and some of the big aerospace companies'

'Really'

'Yes, really. What's going on Lizzie, care to enlighten me. What is a senior government official doing asking a college professor about the two most talked about regions in our Universe.'

'Susie, remember once upon a time you said to me, will you trust me?. Well now it's my turn. Will you trust me Susie?. Say nothing to no one about this, ok?'

'Ok', Susie slowly nodded not taking her eyes off Lizzie.

'Here is my card Susie. Call my personal number that I have written on the back only when you have something. If you do call the office though just say you are an old friend who wants to catch up. I'll come back and collect what you have personally'

'Sure. Any chance you'll tell me more?'

'Possibly, one day maybe'

Lizzie turned to go and as she got to the door Susie called, 'These names on the back of your card. Who are they, what do they mean?'

'I was hoping you could tell me. I think they are all from your field. Can you discreetly look into them please?'

Susie put the card down, walked over and both embraced. There was another jolt although neither wanted to admit it. Lizzie then walked away, twenty years after their last meeting.

Chapter 29

Stevens was exhausted. This was the third time this week Gil had
returned for sexercise, and this had gone on like this for the past
three months. At the end of each day his wristband would buzz
indicating it was his rest period which would normally be it until
breakfast but every other day now his wristband would indicate an
extra half hour of exercise, or as he had dubbed it sexercise.
Tonight, Stevens had actually asked Gil a question during sex.

'How often will we do this?'

'As often as I consider you need it. It is good for you, physically and
mentally. No more talking unless there is something specific you
want'. Gil was naked. She pushed Stevens back onto his bed and
went to work.

Tomorrow he was to be escorted to the flight training area where
he and others are to be introduced to the craft he will eventually
pilot or co pilot through the 'Von Braun' gate. The gate, located off
the edge of Jupiter's secret moon, is named after the famous
German rocket scientist who is alleged to have asked for his body to
be jettisoned towards this Star gate and which has subsequently
been given the German's name. Stevens fell asleep as soon as Gil
left dreaming of a distant planet. A planet he had not set foot on for
over six months. Earth, his planet. One he was struggling to
remember anymore but one he wanted to remember. As his mind
was closing down for rest another planet came into view, darker,
hotter, too hot. Stevens was sweating, gasping for breath. Suddenly
something was around him, all around him. He couldn't see, it was
dark, hot still, then a vision. He was scared now. He didn't want to
go with them, they weren't his kind, no, no, noooo.

Stevens awoke with a start, sweating, breathing heavily. He had been dreaming again. Same dream, same nightmare, 'Fuck'. Perhaps he'll speak to Gil. He wasn't supposed to dream or feel fear in any way. 'What the fuck was going on?'.

His wristband buzzed. Time to get up.

Chapter 30

Lizzie had spent the last week in meeting after meeting. The House Appropriations Committee took up a large part of her time now. Over the last two weeks she had been part of numerous financial discussions ranging from which company should supply government departments with photocopy paper to which pharmaceutical companies can be allowed to bid on supplying lethal drugs to the United States for use in executions. Such meetings, whilst very diverse in nature, can be exhausting. However, each one is necessary.

Kicking her shoes off Lizzie slumped onto her sofa and closed her eyes. It was 8.30 pm and whilst she had not yet eaten yet all she wanted to do was go to bed.

She awoke to the sound of ringing. Her first thought was it must be her daily alarm.

'Hell fire' she muttered to herself jumping up, then immediately realised she was still fully clothed on the sofa. Not again she thought, then shouting at no one in particular she yelled, 'What bloody time is it Cortana?'. Cortana was her virtual house assistant linked to the internet. She had one of these things since their inception a few years ago.

Cortana, in her monotone voice replied, 'It is six fifteen in the morning. It is Sunday, the weather outside is....'

'Enough, stop, Cortana stop' yelled Lizzie.

Who the hell was calling her at 6.15 am on a Sunday, her only day off.

The phone showed UNKNOWN CALLER ID. Lizzie pressed the green accept button and used her official title as she always did for unidentified callers. After all it could be the president. She really hoped not.

'Senator Elizabeth Whitehouse'

'Lizzie, uh....hi, its me, Susie. I'm sorry to call so early but I didn't know what else to do. Its about those names you gave me'.

Lizzie could tell by the short sharp bursts of conversation in between deep breaths that all was not well with Susie.

'Thing is Lizzie, you were right. They were all in the same field as myself. Two I only know by reputation but one I know quite well, in fact he is a friend, I mean, ah, uh.. was. We only spoke a couple of months ago. Well.....thing is, and I don't understand this, but, they're all ah...'

Lizzie already knew what Susie was going to say and cut in loudly to stop her.

'Hey Susie, it's great to hear from you again and it would be nice to have another CATCH UP'. Lizzie emphasised the words catch up as a reminder about her previous request not to divulge anything over the phone.

'Let's catch up properly soon Susie. Are you at home?. I'll ring you back in an hour when we can talk properly. I'm still a little sleepy. Are you ok with that?' again emphasising the last sentence indicating this was not a request but an instruction.

'Thing is Lizzie.....', Susie was persevering and not listening. Lizzie was sharp in tone now,

'Susie, stop, just stop. Where can I reach you, today?'

'I'm at home all day Lizzie, I don't know.....'

'One hour. I will call you back'

Lizzie terminated the call. She showered, threw on some jeans, a pullover, and casual jacket and within ten minutes was looking for a cab. It was 6.40 am on a Sunday morning.

She eventually managed to hail an early cab at the busy Intersection of Kennedy and North Capitol Street, a busy intersection. At 6.55 am Lizzie was walking through the now familiar front door to an innocent looking office in a not so affluent part of DC.

Her new NK13 credit card once again opened the door that no other could.

Pressing the card against the panel on the door to the gate she had a sudden thought.

'Will everyone know where I am going?'. Too late for second thoughts as the door opened and she once again found herself looking at Central Park, New York City.

Walking quickly through Central Park she once again managed to get a cab without any problems. Passing the address to the driver she was at Susie's address precisely forty minutes after they had spoken on the phone this morning.

Walking up the steps to Susie's fashionable Manhattan apartment block she pressed the button against the name Walsh.

No answer.

She pressed again, held it for some time before a response eventually came.

'Hello'

'It's me'

'Sorry, who is it?', Susie sounded nervous.

'It's Lizzie. Susie, open the door'.

'Lizzie, how....what do you mean...are you...'.

Sharp toned now Lizzie gave Susie an instruction.

'Open the fucking door Susie, now, please'. Lizzie was shouting through the speaker.

There was a buzz and Lizzie pushed the outer door open to the apartment block. She took the stairs to the top floor and was greeted at the door by a confused looking Susie who held it open inviting her in.

Closing the door Susie stared at Lizzie.

'We only talked forty minutes ago. You were in DC at 6.15 am. How did you get here so fast?'

'Can't tell you that. It's a government thing'

'What a fast helicopter or something?'

'Doesn't matter, but yes something like that', she lied. 'Now let's sit down, have a cup of coffee and you can tell me why you rang me so early'

Susie went into the kitchen and put the coffee on whilst Lizzie made herself at home.

This was a nice apartment, expensive thought Lizzie to herself. She sat down on what looked like an Italian black leather sofa, under the large bay fronted apartment window. Obviously, the penthouse. Furnished very lavishly. The rug looked Persian, the furniture Italian. Paintings on the wall. They had a familiar look about them, originals no doubt.

Whilst the apartment was furnished to a high standard it was all in a mess. There were papers strewn all over the floor and on the dining table. There were plates with partly eaten food left lying around and cups and glasses everywhere. It looked like Susie had been having a party but Lizzie suspected that this was not the case.

Walking into the living room Susie placed two cups of steaming coffee on the glass topped table. Picking up the half bottle of Jack Daniels and an empty glass she glanced over at Lizzie and spoke softly. 'I needed to calm myself down'

'Why, tell me'

Susie grabbed an ash tray from the littered dining table and lit up a cigarette.

This was worrying thought Lizzie.

'Well. Those names you gave me. Well, I did what you asked. I researched, printed the information off on Lyra and Zeta then summarised it all for you so that it would make some sense to you'

'Thanks'.

Susie took a drag on the cigarette before continuing.

'It's ok. It's my subject. Anyway I did some research on the names, one of which I know fairly well and they were all....ah'

'Dead'

Susie looked up startled. Quickly inhaling on the cigarette again.

'How did you know Lizzie?'

'I didn't but I was just trying to put two and two together. Your anxious state, the telephone call, the liquor, mess everywhere. Not like you is it'

Susie had tears in her eyes as she continued.

'One of them was a friend of mine, a bit obsessive, but still a good friend and colleague. Lars, Lars Holman, Norwegian American. We spoke about two months ago. I spent a couple of weeks at his winter retreat in Oslo last January. Taught me to ski you know'

'I'm sorry Susie'

'The Police said he had taken his own life. But that can't be true. I mean, why would he?'

'I don't know. Perhaps he had worries. Worries you were not aware of. Wife trouble?, husband trouble?, who knows'

'He didn't have anyone. No parents alive, no siblings, no partner I was aware of. He was married to his work. That's what he always said'

'And the other names?'

'Well, again, both deceased. I've only checked via the web and their University but I can get Martin to ring the Police tomorrow. They both took their own lives too apparently. Strange don't you think?'

'What was Lars obsessed with?'

Susie was staring and seemed not to hear. Standing now she was looking beyond Lizzie out through the bay window at the early Manhattan skyline.

'Martin also made a call you know. To an old university friend of his in DC. A journalist, but one with a passion for astronomy. An amateur really, but only because that was his choice. He was very well informed'

'Uh huh'

'Thing is, his name is Henry by the way, Henry Hanna. Thing is, Martin saw me working on this research and called his friend Henry to ask him if he had heard of these other two Astronomers'

Lizzie sat up now, concern on her face. 'You should not have asked him to do that Susie. I told you this was confidential'

'Thing is Martin called him and he said he would call back. But he didn't. Martin tried calling again but couldn't get hold of him on the phone. His email had an 'out of office' on it so he called his newspaper.'

'And?'

'He's dead. Same as the others. Taken his own life they said. What the fuck is going on Lizzie?'

Lighting up another cigarette Susie was crying now, uncontrollably.

Lizzie was short and sharp, voice raised.

'What was Lars obsessed with Susie?. You said he had an obsession'.

'Yes, he did. They all did. They all had the same obsession'

'Which is?. Tell me Susie'

'Aliens. Fucking Aliens Lizzie, and Antarctica'

Chapter 31

Inside the craft the following names were inscribed on what looked like a metal plate next to the cockpit entrance. This must be their craft. This was assigned to them, the final team.

STEVENS (PILOT)

BROTHERTON (CO PILOT)

HAYES (FLIGHT ENGINEER)

OLSEN (LINGUIST)

PARKER (SECURITY)

CONNORS (SECURITY)

GIL - Genetically Induced Lifeform (MEDICAL, TECHNICAL, CAPTAIN)

Stevens had trained for three months solid now but only on simulators. As a trained Pilot he knew the value of simulators but also that they could only prepare you so much. It was nothing like the real thing.

As he sat in the Pilot seat next to Brotherton, who took the seat to the right, it dawned on him that he was about to take control of a spacecraft. He was about to take a flight into the blackness that was the cosmos, space.

They were team 3 for Zeta, at least that was how they had been addressed on a number of occasions.

Team 1 had apparently recently proceeded through 'The Gate'. Team 2 would follow in the coming weeks. Team 3, his team, would follow team 2 and were scheduled to enter The Gate in approximately six weeks if the training went according to plan.

The craft itself was not saucer shaped as Stevens had expected but was more of a Stealth shape. In fact, it was a flying triangle. Three equal sides, a dull metallic silver grey in colour with no obvious windows when looking from the outside. There were no markings that Stevens could see on first glimpse but like everything else he had learned, that meant nothing. As they were escorted to the hold of the mother ship Stevens was now getting a much closer look. Each side of the triangular vessel was about thirty meters in length. Running his hand over the surface it wasn't as smooth as it looked, definitely more like a fine sandpaper texture. Gil took the whole team around the ship which was being held off the ground by three columns. The columns reminded Stevens of ancient Roman structures which dropped away for some considerable distance below the craft. The team were walking along a hanging metallic walkway which surrounded the craft and looked like it could itself be retracted. It also linked them to the engineering bay. This holding area held about fifteen other identical craft. Stevens tried to count them but was ushered along by Gil. There were also numerous empty areas where craft had clearly been held but were no longer there anymore.

Gil spoke.

'Yes, we did have fifty of these 'Gateway craft'. We now have sixteen left. When we set off on our journey there will be eight left on board. Today will be the first of many test flights before our transition flight. Any questions before we embark?'.

There were no questions. The team were all still awestruck by the sight of the craft. In a more commanding tone Gil continued. Touching something on her belt her voice sounded amplified.

'Let's go'

All six immediately turned and followed Gil across the hanging walkways. Instead of leading them inside the craft she abruptly stood to one side.

'Stevens, you enter first. Stand in front of me and face the craft'

Stevens did as he was told. He felt compelled in some way. As he faced the ship, he was still amazed to look at the dull metallic grey exterior of this magnificent flying craft. Looking closer now he saw that it was not in fact a triangle but more of a squashed pyramid. It had three sides that all rose to a central point. He was looking at the back of the craft. Even though each side looked the same he somehow knew he was looking at the back. Was Gil speaking to his subconscious again?. He didn't know. He couldn't see any markings at first but a voice in his head was telling him to look closer. He did, concentrating hard. All of a sudden, the markings appeared, obvious when you knew where to look. Or were they only apparent when you wanted to see them? They were not the usual markings on craft he had flown with the military. These were marked with symbols. They looked like mathematical symbols mixed with Egyptian hieroglyphics. Stevens noticed at least seven symbols in varying combinations but nothing in his head translated their meaning at present.

'Stevens. Board the craft'

Gil was speaking to him but all he could do was stare at the craft. He was about to ask how when Gil spoke again.

'Think about boarding. Tell the craft what you want to do. With your mind'

There was a ten meter gap between the walkway and craft. The drop in between was over twenty meters. Not life threatening but one likely to cause injury. Stevens closed his eyes and concentrated. He really wanted to board this craft. He imagined a walkway leading from where he was stood to the ship. With eyes still closed Stevens heard some gasps from behind. Opening his eyes, he could not believe what was in front of him. A walkway appeared to be in place. It extended from the craft towards him.

'Stevens, continue. Team 3 follow Stevens into the craft'.

'Continue to concentrate Stevens, this is real'.

Stevens did as he was instructed. He took a step onto the narrow grey ramp leading towards the craft. It was solid as he took a tentative first step. Obviously metallic but it made no sound on impact with his feet. It was a meter or so wide, no handrails. Stevens stood upright and walked towards the entrance. As he neared the entrance he could see the symbols more clearly, a different shade of grey. Grey on grey but easily visible somehow. Standing now at the crafts entrance Stevens stopped momentarily then stepped through the seamless opening.

Stepping through into darkness Stevens whispered to himself, 'Lights would be good'.

As if by magic everything was illuminated. Lights everywhere.

All six gathered inside what looked like a decompression chamber but much larger. Gil followed the team in.

'You will see there are seven flight suits hanging on the walls behind us. One for each of us. We will put them on here, now. Leave your non flight clothing in the compartments behind the suits.

The suits were all hanging as Gil had said. Their names were displayed above them and were also emblazoned on their left breast above a very strange looking badge. Stevens found his next to Brotherton's. The suit was hanging on what looked like a plastic mannequin. It reminded Stevens of the mannequins that were displayed in sports shops. Looking at his name displayed on the suit he saw that below it was displayed a selection of symbols, like those displayed on the outer skin of the ship.

Looking around he saw that Gil was nearly into her suit with most of the others close behind her. Taking off his garments he quickly started to pull on the suit. As he began stretching the material Gil called over, 'Nothing underneath. You must be naked'. Reluctantly Stevens removed his underwear and stood there in all his glory and began to pull on the suit, once again. More like a surfers wetsuit, it took some pulling on with each arm and leg needing some strenuous pulling for the suit to fully cover the whole body. There was a zipper that ran diagonally from the left hip to the right shoulder.

Gil faced them and spoke. 'The zippers once pulled to complete the suit will trigger the life support processor within each suit. You will feel a slight tingling sensation as the suit hooks into your body. The suit will be one with you, another layer of skin. It will become part of your body. Pull the zippers like this'.

Gil pulled her zipper across her body from her left hip all the way to her right shoulder. There was a subtle noise, a click or perhaps a snap of some kind as Gil visibly stiffened. Then the suit seemed to illuminate briefly. Millions of miniscule lights seemed to flicker briefly as if Gil became luminescent, and then, all of a sudden, they went out.

'The first time is the worst gentlemen. Activate your suits now'

Stevens pulled the zipper across his body, tentatively. The suit felt soft on the inside whilst the outside felt smooth, in a metallic kind of way. As Stevens pulled the zipper the last few inches the suit became tighter. It felt more like an extra layer of skin than a garment to be worn. As the zipper reached its terminal point Stevens heard the 'click' and knew it had reached the docking point.

'On your left thigh gentlemen there is a colour keypad. RED, GREEN, YELLOW, and BLUE. A primary colour code. This is your suits colour coded locking mechanism. You will now input a four point colour code by simply touching the keypad. Any order, any colour, same or different. Your choice, but after this first time the same code must be input each time the suit is activated. This is your personal code. Everyone indicate to me you understand'.

All nodded.

'Input the code now and the suit will be activated'

There was general hesitation from the whole team, so Stevens took a step forward.

'Ok, here goes'

Stevens touched the keypad for times. The pad itself was the size of a dollar bill but square in shape split into four, each quarter displaying a primary colour. Stevens pressed RED, BLUE, RED, BLUE simply because they were the top two colours and should he be in a rush, this would be easy to reach and remember. That was his logic anyway. As he told himself this there was a sudden bolt of electricity that continued through his whole body. He visibly stiffened. It was a hot and cold tingling sensation like nothing he had ever felt before. Thousands of small needles throughout the suit and a thousand times thinner than a human hair had pierced his skin. Stevens gasped, 'Whoa', arching his back. It was pain mixed with pleasure. That was the only way to describe the feeling. Within three seconds however it was gone. He stood amazed at the fluorescent nature of the suit. As he moved his legs and arms the suit gave off an electrical charge. There was an ethereal aura about the suit. Stevens felt it was weirdly wonderful.

'Ok everyone. Do as Stevens has done. You can see from his reaction that there is a strange sensation, but this will not last. It will also fade with each time you put on the suit. Remember your codes. You will need to remember them to deactivate the suit and take it off'.

Hayes stopped just as he was about to touch the keypad.

'What if we forget the code'

Gil was cold in her response.

'The suit stays on. Eventually you will die'

Hayes was obviously unimpressed. 'Great. And if we put the wrong code in?'

Gil replied in a cold tone as before, rather matter of fact, 'That does not matter. Its the sequence that counts'

'Fine, here goes then'

Stevens watched the engineer closely. He needed this guy to be strong and level headed. Going into space was difficult enough. Without an engineer on top of his game would be suicide.

Hayes tapped the colour code. RED, BLUE, YELLOW, GREEN. He immediately stiffened and gasped, 'Shee...it'. Then 'wow!', 'That was pretty good', as if he had actually enjoyed it.

There were other gasps and plenty of expletives from the rest of the group, all except the security guys, who seemed to take it all in their stride. Stevens watched Parker as he zipped up his suit. There was no gasp, not much of a stiffening and an almost immediate return to normal. It was much the same as when Gil had put hers on. Stevens thought this was strange but then most infantry, especially special forces, were a little strange. Stevens dismissed his reaction as nothing out of the ordinary for a grunt and thought no more of it. When the whole team had settled into their suits Gil spoke again.

'Connors close the outer door'

Connors turned and walked towards the crafts doorway. He was clearly looking for a switch. Stevens knew he wouldn't find one.

'No Connors. You must close it with your mind. Focus on the doorway and visualise it is closed.

Connors turned towards the door. At first nothing. The doorway and gantry remained open and still in place. Then, in an instant there was no opening in the craft wall. Connors walked over to where the doorway had once been. Nothing, it was seamless. He ran his hand over the interior where the opening had once been. As he did this a glow appeared under his hand. Where his hand made contact with the interior wall a luminescence appeared, albeit for a brief nano second. For that very brief moment Connors felt he could see through the wall as if it became transparent.

Gil again, 'Mr Parker, your turn. Take us through to the main body of this craft. Open the inner doorway'

Parker for some reason did not hesitate. He appeared to have no trouble at all with this instruction. Stevens noticed that he didn't even look towards the chamber door. He just smiled, 'No problem Gil' and the interior door slid to one side.

'In true Star Trek style', he mused to Stevens as they all walked through the hatch into a short gangway leading to what Stevens assumed was the flight deck. Only it wasn't the flight deck. At least it certainly didn't look like any flight deck he had experienced thus far. More like a mini cinema the seats were all arranged in a 'V' formation with Gil taking the rear seat at the pointed end. In front of her to the right and left were the Pilot and Co Pilot respectively. In front of the Co Pilot sat the Linguist. In front of the Pilot sat the Engineer, and taking up the front two edges of the 'V' were the two Security guys.

'Your seats are clearly marked gentlemen. The only difference to the simulators you have been training on is the seat alignment and the surroundings. Each console is exactly the same as your training console'.

A slight pause as each team member took up their position.

'We are sat in an inverted 'V' formation. A strong symbolic alignment. It is also regarded as a friendly sign. Everything else will be familiar to you'

As Stevens sat, he did indeed realise that all was exactly the same as the simulators.

'This first expedition is putting your training into practice. You each have your roles within the team. This is the beginning of the end gentlemen. Our destination, your destiny, awaits us all. Let us proceed'.

Stevens only registered part of this Captains speech. He was still thinking about the inverted V symbol and knew all too well the meaning. All through history the V and inverted V were signs associated with military. Often described as the sword and chalice they were long since regarded and used in military circles from early Roman times. Only problem Stevens could see was that they were not actually sat in an inverted V, simply a V formation.

As he pondered this Stevens realised that he knew exactly what his role was. He knew what everyone's roles were apart from the security guys. Stevens attention was abruptly brought back to the here and now as Gil spoke again.

'Stevens, please take control of the craft and prepare to take us into orbit around Titan. This is our next step towards the 'Van Braun Gate' and our eventual Interstellar journey'.

Stevens placed both his palms onto the screen in front of him which illuminated and suddenly became one with Stevens. As Stevens brain started to integrate with the flight systems computer his and all other chairs started to rotate. Stevens found himself facing the opposite way and now realised that he was indeed positioned in an inverted 'V' with Gill ahead of him at the sharp end and the security guys at the back.

The training in the simulators had not prepared Stevens for what he was looking at. Space, stars, a distant planet, no two. The whole of the back wall, which was now the front was transparent. It looked as if there was nothing there. As if the front of the ship was missing.

'Mr Stevens', Gil commanded.

'Acknowledged', and with nothing more than a slight vibration Stevens was at one with the flight system and the ship had disengaged and was moving. The screen in front or whatever it was proved it, the planet they could all see was getting closer. The leviathan that was the planet Saturn was filling the screen. He could hear some gasps and heavy breathing coming from behind, but he had not the time or inclination to turn around. He was focussed on the little moon just coming into view in the south east.

Titan was approaching.

As Stevens took the ship toward Titan and orbit GIL spoke to the team.

'We are approaching Titan, the largest moon of Saturn. The only moon known to have a dense atmosphere, and the only known body in space, other than Earth, where clear evidence of stable bodies of surface liquid have been found in our Solar System'.

'This is a planet-like moon and is 50% larger in diameter than Earth's moon and 80% more massive. It is primarily composed of ice and rocky material, which is likely differentiated into a rocky core surrounded by various layers of ice, and a subsurface layer of ammonia-rich liquid water. It is a mineral rich planet and one that we have visited many times before. It's atmosphere is largely nitrogen, with methane and ethane also prevalent but the Secret Space Program has, through it's atmospheric engineering program, been preparing Titan for re-colonization for over two decades. The climate—including wind and rain—creates surface features similar to those of Earth, such as dunes, rivers, lakes, seas and deltas, and is dominated by seasonal weather patterns as on Earth. This moon will be the final resting place for many of the ship's inhabitants, but not for us. This is just a drop off, then off to Jupiter and through the gate'.

Chapter 32

As soon as Lizzie had left Susie, she had resolved to find out more about these individuals Susie claimed were dead, murdered apparently. Ok so she wasn't surprised that some of Susie's friends had an interest in Science, astronomy, aliens even, but she did find it hard to believe that her government would knowingly murder their citizens for being Alien believers. For goodness sake she now believed they existed herself. No, she knew they existed. Surely disclosing the existence of aliens was no longer that much of an issue. The massive public spending however, the systematic theft of taxpayers money to fund research into space and alien technology. Now that is an issue that Lizzie could not leave alone.

And this business about Antarctica. Why is that so important?. Lizzie was determined to find out. She was not going to sign any more cheques for secret government spending without good reason and certainly not without more answers. If she didn't get the answers then maybe the time was right for her to disclose to the public exactly where all their money was going and perhaps re channel it elsewhere.

That was last week. Since then she had been phoning, e mailing, even knocking on the doors of some very senior Department of Defence officials, Intelligence agency officials, and NASA officials, asking some very awkward questions about finance, black operations, secret space missions, and America's policy on executing military personnel. In fact, she had requested from the department of defence a list of all personnel who had been executed in the past ten years. Families have a right to know the truth about their loved ones.

So far, she had not received any responses at all.

Lizzie picked up the phone and called Susie in New York. The phone went to answerphone with the same message she had heard for the last three days, 'Hi we can't get to the phone right now. Please leave a number and we might, yes that's what I said, might, get back to you'.

At first Lizzie found the message amusing but now having heard it at least a dozen times it wasn't funny anymore. This time Lizzie was angry and left another but less friendly message.

'For goodness sake Susie, I can't help you if you don't pick up the phone. I need some more information about Lars and Henry, this Henry Hanna bloke, please......'

Then the phone tone changed, there was a beep and silence.

Lizzie listened. She could almost feel someone was on the line but not speaking.

'Susie, is this you'

'Susie is unavailable', a man's voice but not one Lizzie recognised. The phone was making clicking noises in the background, the line not very good.

'Sorry, who are you?', Lizzie questioned.

The man again, a deep voice, too deep, masked maybe.

'Susie is not here. Stop calling, and stop investigating. No more warnings Miss Whitehouse'

'Hey, its Senator White......', then the phone went dead before she could finish.

Lizzie dialled the number again and the line went to a continuous tone.

'Fuck', screamed Lizzie.

Her internal buzzer indicating her personal assistant had a call waiting sounded.

'Hi Trish, who is it?'

'Lizzie it's the Police, they would like to speak to you'

'What do the DC cops want, did they say?'

'Uh, no they didn't. They would not go into detail only that it was important they speak directly with you. Oh, and it's not the DC cops, it's the New York Cops. The NYPD are on the line'

'Ok Trish put them through'

For some reason which Lizzie couldn't put her finger on she had a bad feeling. She did not want to take this call. She somehow knew it was bad news coming.

'Hello Senator Whitehouse speaking. How can I help you?'.

Three minutes after putting the NYPD through to her boss Trish went running into the adjoining office. She heard a scream that sounded like a wounded animal and rushing through the door she found the Senator on her knees behind her desk sobbing. The phone was still in her hand and stretched to breaking point from its origin which was hanging over the other side of the desk.

Trish went over and knelt beside Lizzie. Placing one arm around her shoulders she took the phone from her hand, checked there was no longer a connection and then replaced it in the cradle.

Trish was fairly new to the Senators staff and whilst she did not know her well, as far as she knew there was no partner or family so any bad news could only be friends or colleagues.

'Is everything alright?'. Trish regretted this question as soon as it was uttered. Of course everything was not ok.

'Can I get you anything?. Do you want to tell me what's happened?'

'No but I am going to tell the whole fucking world about what's going on with this Planet'

Standing up Lizzie had obviously pulled herself together. She had a strange look in her eyes, thoughts of total disclosure going through her head. Trish thought she looked pale when she had first entered but now the Senator looked flushed. She was angry.

'Leave me', Lizzie barked at Trish. 'No callers and I am not to be disturbed, understand?'

'Yes ma'am'

Trish knew there was a minor official due to arrive this afternoon wanting to discuss educational funding for the coming year. Trish began to ask, 'Mr Kowalski is due at....'

'No disturbances'

Trish nodded, turned and left the Senators office closing the door behind her.

Returning to her desk Trish opened up the Outlook calendar and found the contact for Kowalski's office. She would call and re arrange this meeting as best she could. First though she needed to make an urgent call. Picking up the phone she punched in a telephone number that she had memorised. It was answered almost immediately.

'Yes'

'I've been told to report anything strange. Well I have just witnessed Senator Whitehouse acting very strange.'

Chapter 33

Travelling at light speed was theoretically possible but not as yet physically achievable. Stevens had been piloting the craft on practice sorties for weeks and had completed eight test flights. He was piloting the craft using his consciousness. The craft had dual controls in that it could be manually operated by another member of the team but only insofar as being able to use the computer controls to put the ship back into an autopilot mode with a selected destination.

Only Stevens, and Brotherton as the co-pilot, can actually fly the craft using their consciousness and Brotherton can only step into the consciousness of the craft if Stevens is no longer conscious.

For this reason, Brotherton has taken his practice flights when Stevens has not been inside the craft and has sometimes flown with other crews from the mothership.

Stevens, Brotherton, and other pilots had been summoned to a location within the mothership they had not been before.

The room once again was dark, and each individual was once again plugged into a body formed seat.

GIL appeared and the screen behind her came to life.

'To reach our destination we must all focus on our consciousness and the point at which we want to be. We live within a frequency band, vibration and mathematics are the key'.

'Tesla was right, we have access to infinite amounts of energy. Energy you are about to access with the mathematics of life, the mathematics of the universe. Look at the numbers on the screen, focus on them. Focus. Do the math'.

Stevens felt a sharp prick, and felt a liquid enter both his right thigh and left arm. It was like a bolt of lightning. Stevens was indeed focussed on the screen. The numbers were alive. His brain began to do the math. He read the numbers, 1,2,3,4,5,6,7,8,9.

They were sequenced around a clock face. A pattern appeared. Stevens could see it clearly.

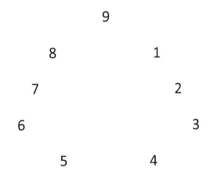

The numbers appeared to be talking to Stevens.

1 times 1 equals 1 . 2 times 2 equals 4, doubling again equals 8, then 16. 1 plus 6 equals 7.

16 doubled gives 32, 3 plus 2 equals 5. It went on and on. Doubling up then adding the digits always came in as 1,2, 4,8, 7, or 5.

It went on and on but always the number digits added to give the above whilst the numbers 3,6, and 9 had an even more unique relationship.

Stevens was in a state he could not explain. The numbers were the answer. He was accessing a new dimension, the fourth dimension. Numbers. Vibration, and energy. A creative melting pot.

Stevens continued to focus. 3 doubles to equal 6. Double again for 12. Add 1 plus 2 is 3. !2 doubled is 24, then 48, 96, 192. Whatever you double up to 3, 6, and 9 is always the answer. The frequency of the universe.

It goes on ad infinitum. Mathematics can take you anywhere in the universe. Tesla was right. Mathematics is the universal language of the Universe. Everywhere in the Universe obeys the law of mathematics.

As Stevens mind raced through the ever increasing numbers, their meaning became clear. A roadmap was taking form. There was no need for faster than light travel to reach their destination. The numbers would take them to Zeta.

Stevens lost consciousness, or did he in fact reach a different level of consciousness within a new dimension. The numbers in his head, his mind, his consciousness, took him to another location. Stevens came to. He was still sat, fixed into his seat, but he was now sat in the craft alongside Brotherton.

Each training sortie went this way. Stevens lost consciousness as he knew it and swam in a sea of numbers. Numbers, he realised were the key and could take him anywhere and to any time.

Stevens was sat at the console again, with Brotherton at his side.

His consciousness was at a different level. Each training session Stevens attended his consciousness seemed to transform to a higher level. This was the last session before the final approach to Zeta. The numbers were everywhere, the whole universe was a sea of numerical digits. The whole fabric of the universe was mathematics. Stevens was in a state of consciousness that was neither human or physical. He was digital. He could see and be everywhere at any time, now, past, and future. Stevens was swimming through time. He was moving ahead, could see the journey he was on. The journey he was going to take. Stevens pushed on, he could experience the future, touch it.

Then, nothing. The journey would end. It was finite. Time was finite. A strange feeling overcame Stevens, even in this enhanced state. A feeling of unease.

Travelling back now, into his past. He saw his own execution, experienced it again, his birth, his parents, his grandparents. His grandfather, an engineer. A revelation. His own grandfather was a member of the Secret Space Program. Stevens could see his grandfather working, in Area 51. He watched his grandfather, sat in front of his television set at home. A message, a warning was needed. Stevens crossed the barrier of time and placed a message onto a television screen. A message from the future. A warning from the future to change the past. To save them all.

Then, like before, everything started to become grey, foggy. Stevens was being disconnected remotely. Tunnel vision, then, suddenly sat back at the console next to an equally bewildered Brotherton, on the ship's flight deck.

Gil spoke, 'Are you ready Stevens?'.

Initially hesitating, trying to remember why he was uneasy, Stevens eventually replied,

'I'm ready', as Gil approached him, looking at him.

'Good. Next stop Zeta. No deviations. Understand?'

Stevens nodded as Gil, still staring straight at him, spoke again.

'Brotherton. You are on standby'.

GiL was behind them, along with the rest of the team.

GIL spoke again, 'Prepare to leave the mothership. Our final journey is about to begin'.

Stevens spoke, 'Understood'.

Brotherton followed, 'Understood'.

A hologram appeared in front of the two pilots depicting their current position and their destination. As Stevens body integrated with the ship's conscious controls the hologram changed from a visual representation of their journey to numbers, sets of numbers, Tesla's vortex of numbers.

The craft moved and Stevens engaged the drive pulling away from the mothership and accelerating through space at an astonishing rate. The crew were mesmerised and sat in awe at the screen in front. Flashes of light were there then gone, the craft moving through space and time in a way they were not expecting.

Stevens was now engulfed by the hologram. He was inside a sea of numbers, his consciousness linking with each and every one. Stevens did not see any of the ship's journey, he was at a level of consciousness required to be at a point in space and time whilst also at another point, every point in space and time at once. Stevens was not physical anymore, he was at a level he did not understand, conscious of himself, but not in a physical form. He was experiencing the mathematics, the numbers, each doubling giving him a new meaning. Then, he saw the number he needed to experience to reach their destination. Numbers truly were the fabric of the universe. They linked into everything. Everything was mathematics, an equation, a program that can be solved to take us anywhere.

Stevens experienced something and understood he had solved a puzzle, reached a point, completed a journey. Then another jolt and Stevens became aware of his physical being once more. He felt an inner peace, a feeling of tranquillity. Until he opened his eyes.

The sight in front of him was out of this world. He was now looking at another world. Stevens had somehow piloted the ship to their destination.

The hologram in front was now indicating the craft was in orbit around a planet in a binary star system. They had arrived at their destination.

A voice from somewhere, 'Welcome to Zeta'.

'This is a binary star system and you will see there are two planets here. We are approaching Zeta 1, our final destination. Other teams are here. More will soon be arriving at Zeta 2. You have travelled thirty nine light years, an unimaginable distance'.

The crew were stood, only Stevens and Brotherton were still sat as they disengaged themselves from their integrated seats. The crew, along with GIL were looking at the picture through the crafts front screen. A planet, not unlike Earth, but with two Sun's in the distance. Other craft were also in orbit, hundreds of them, all shapes and sizes, all heading towards a giant mothership who appeared to be devouring the craft as they approached.

Brotherton spoke, 'Now what?'

Chapter 34

It was a little overcast, damp, but not wet. A chilly breeze swept through the cemetery, but Lizzie felt nothing.

It had been two weeks now since Suzie's death and she was still in shock. Or was it anger, yes that was it, she was angry, very, very, angry. She wanted someone to give her answers and she wanted them fast. Someone was going to pay.

Susie didn't die. She was murdered. Lizzie knew the coincidences all pointed to one thing. A conspiracy of monumental proportions involving governments, multi national corporations, the military, big Industrial giants that were household names, the film industry, the fucking lot.

Lizzie was whispering to herself, 'Aliens, For fuck sake, Aliens'.

A tap on her elbow from the old lady sat beside her, 'Sorry dear what was that?'

It was Susie's mother. She held a red tulip, Susie's favourite flower. Standing up now, along with a couple of dozen other mourners, words were being spoken by a man in a white smock. Lizzie didn't know Susie was a Catholic. Lizzie stood and whispered to the old lady again, 'Who arranged all this?, it's really lovely. I didn't realise Susie was so religious'.

She whispered back, 'She wasn't Elizabeth dear, but her kind colleagues wouldn't let me pay a penny. There they are'. The old lady pointing towards two men stood in the distance. Two men, dark glasses, long trench coats. Government men. Then a third, stood amongst the group on the opposite side of the hole that Susie was now being lowered into. Smaller, dressed similar, but unmistakeable. It was Aldrin.

'Fuck this', retorted Lizzie before walking off as the congregation continued to sing the Lords Prayer.

Lizzie was in full stride, almost running now as she began to put a brief but effective plan into place. Reaching her car out of breath, she took out her mobile phone and scrawled through her contacts until she found who she was looking for.

'Hi it's Lizzie, Lizzie Whitehouse. Yes, that's correct, the very same. I need to meet urgently. I may need your help with something, and this will certainly help you with your disclosure program'.

Lizzie listened to the voice on the other end, then interrupted them in mid flow.

'No, this is a one time offer. You come to the address I will text you tonight at 7pm. This cannot wait Mr Freer. 7pm tonight understand'. Before any response she terminated the call.

As she opened the car door another black sedan pulled alongside. The rear window wound down and a voice called out from within. ' Do not do this Miss Whitehouse. Now is not the time. There will be consequences'.

The window wound back up and the car moved away. The face inside, pale, gaunt, long white hair, unusual white clothing, ethnic style. Lizzie recalled that initial meeting with the group. The man spoke but his lips did not move. It was him again. Another warning.

Lizzie started her car and sped off out of the cemetery more determined than ever.

Chapter 35

Lizzie was sat at a large round conference table at the rear meeting room of a small downtown Legal office. She had called in another favour. Lizzie looked round the room, a very familiar room. She had so many stories to tell, this room had even more stories to tell, some happy, most sad, but it brought back memories of a time which seemed such an age away. An altogether happier time in her life. The problems were everyone else's and she sought to help others. Now, sat at the mahogany table, she needed help from others.

A knock on the conference room door brought Lizzie back to the present.

'In here' replied Lizzie.

The door opened and in walked the man she was expecting. Something of a celebrity amongst conspiracy theorists, Ufologists, and the Alien disclosure community. A qualified dentist who was practising until ten years ago, he now worked full time on his Alien disclosure project and a free clean energy quest for the planet.

58 years old, physically fit, lean and toned, he looked like a man who not only looked after himself but someone who may have had some surgical work done.

Lizzie stood, walked to greet him and held out her hand. 'Thank you for coming Mr Freer'.

He took her hand and gave it a gentle shake, 'You didn't really give me any choice'.

'Please sit down, I have things I wish to disclose to you. Some you may be aware of, some I'm sure you suspect, most I'm sure will astonish you'.

Freer took a seat on the comfortable leather sofa to one side. Lizzie collected the papers she had spread on the conference table and took a seat opposite.

Lizzie looked into Freer's eyes. He seemed a little uncomfortable.

She spoke first, 'What do you really know about the Secret Space Program Mr Freer?'

'I have briefed every President since Reagan on the existence of extra terrestrial life and it's implications for future life on Earth Miss Whitehouse. It's real and I have lobbied every government to release more information, which they do, but only as a drip feed to the population'.

'And the Secret Space Program, Solar Warden, colonization of other planets. What do you know about this?'

'Well, after the Roswell incident in forty seven, our technology has developed exponentially as I'm sure we have back engineered what was recovered. Rumours of some other recoveries of downed craft around the world persist and I'm also sure we are flying around the skies and probably even into Earth orbit more than we the public, are aware of. As far as Solar Warden goes, then I have never seen proof this program exists. I ask again Miss Whitehouse, why am I here?'

Lizzie put down several bundles of paper in front of Freer. 'Take a look at these Mr Freer'.

Freer picked up the first sheet which was marked 'TOP SECRET DEPARTMENT OF CORRECTIONS'.

There was a list of names and execution dates.

The dates were all from the previous two years and alongside the name of each individual was listed their rank or position, role, Military Unit or organisation.

Freer read, 'Can I take photos?'.

'These are for you Mr Freer'

'So, this list of executed personnel, nearly all are military with some scientists. Very strange, I didn't realise the Military executed personnel anymore'

'There are profiles for every one of them Mr Freer. Read them and you will see they are all the very best in their field'

'I don't understand'

'Don't you. Just read on'. Lizzie got up from the sofa and returned to sit at the conference table. Taking out her mobile she began to look through her recent emails. Freer read on, obviously engrossed as Lizzie replied to her ever increasing mail box.

Freer read on. Thirty minutes later he raised his head.

'Okay, so am I reading this and making up the answers here which I find that even I cannot believe'

'Tell me what you think you are looking at Mr Freer'

'Let's say that these execution lists are in fact true. There are several names I have found from the first list copied onto the second batch of papers which are headed, OFF WORLD CREW'

'Uh huh'

'They in turn seem to connect to a list of Navy battleships, which I have never heard of, USSS Brewster, USSS Alden, USSS Winslow. What is the connection here?'

'You are correct to link them and if you look deeper into the lists, with some further investigation, you will see that all of the executed persons are linked in some way to these ships'.

'Please go on Senator'

'Well, these are ships indeed, ships that very few American citizens are aware of. The names themselves relate to the first settlers in America well over two hundred years ago. They are named after the first colonists that arrived on the shores of the USA, passengers from one of the most famous ships.....'

'The Mayflower'

'Correct Mr Freer, but these ships are not ocean going ships'

'Then what are they?. You don't mean....'

'Indeed I do. They are Space Ships Mr Freer, already built and in service. They have been for some time. The USSS relates to the UNITED STATES SECRET SPACE program'

'So, it exists'

'Absolutely'

'And what do you want me to do with this information Senator?'

Freer was a little too calm as he stood from the sofa thought Lizzie. She sensed a change. Was it fear? No, he was very calm as if this information was not a complete revelation.

'I want you to help me disclose everything Mr Freer, and I mean everything. To the public, to those government officials who do not know, media organisations, the scientific community, total disclosure along with the accounts for which I currently have to sign off. Trillions of American taxpayer dollars, every year, diverted away from the general public to black operations and the military'

Freer was paying too much attention to his phone and not paying enough attention to what she was saying.

He was looking directly at her again. Lizzie found his look unsettling.

'Did you hear what I said Mr Freer?. Or have I disclosed things that even you cannot believe?'

The door to the office slowly opened and the doorway framed an instantly recognisable figure.

'He already knows all this Lizzie'

Aldrin strode into the room and took a seat at the conference table.

'How the hell did you get in here?', Lizzie screamed at Aldrin. She was shifting her glare between both men, face reddening with anger. More footsteps, then men in uniform, a military uniform, walked in. They took up a position behind, at both sides, and in front of Lizzie.

Freer walked from the room and left Lizzie alone with Aldrin and the military.

'You were warned Lizzie. There is an agenda to all this and I'm afraid you do not set that agenda. You are a part of it. Or I should say, you were a part of it. Take her'

Lizzie tried to protest but before any sound could escape her mouth there was a cold feeling in her neck, just below the base of her skull. She was stood motionless, could not move but was being held up by two of the men in uniform. She could hear, see, her brain had consciousness but could not function physically. She was trapped inside her head. She started to scream inside that head as the men physically carried her from the office into an awaiting ambulance parked out the rear.

Being placed on the gurney, strapped in place, she screamed again as another military unit injected her with a clear liquid. This time into her arm. Slowly, she stopped screaming and drifted off into darkness.

Aldrin gave some instructions to the uniforms in the conference room before leaving via the back door to the small downtown legal practice.

Freer was waiting in the rear alleyway with two other uniforms.

'Thank you, Mr Freer'

'Thank you. And your side of the bargain'

'Yes, as agreed you will receive full disclosure and a very large investment for your company. You will need to sign the Official Secrets Act of course'

'Of course'

'Then let's get that done Mr Freer'

Chapter 36

Lizzie awoke slowly to a darkened environment. A hospital perhaps, had she been injured?.

There were tubes entering her left and right arms, another directly into an artery in her neck. A monitor of sorts was attached to her chest whilst an uncomfortable feeling between her legs confirmed it. She had been catheterised.

Lizzie was conscious and the darkness was slowly becoming clearer. What sort of hospital was this?. A conversation she had recently niggled at her as she attempted to recall it.

An attempt to move was fruitless. She could not move anything, arms, legs, even her head would not budge. Panic started to set in. If Lizzie could, she would have screamed. The plastic tube entering her mouth and throat prevented this. Lizzie started to panic feeling the head restraint tighten as she tried to lift her head. The panic was only momentary as the initial panic was soon replaced by an inner calmness. Lizzie could feel the restraints tighten around her ankles, wrists, and thighs at any attempt at movement.

There was a sudden bleep and some motion around her scalp. The head restraint was retracting giving her some head movement.

The room was dimly lit and she was lying horizontally on some sort of gurney still. Looking down Lizzie saw she was dressed in a silver grey all in one suit. A zipper went from her left shoulder down to her right thigh. A badge was emblazoned on her left breast. It was round and looked like a planet, no the moon, with some sort of spaceship in orbit. On her right breast there were two big letters, G and P, GP.

Lizzie slowly moved her head to her left and was taken aback . Tears began to flow and at that moment Lizzie longed to drift back in time to happier times, to her childhood. If the drugs had not been reacting to her bodily requirements, she would have been terrified by what she was looking at. Row upon row of people. All lying still on gurney's, attached to monitors with a variety of tubes entering their bodies. Men, women, all races, oh god no, some small gurney's, not children please. Calmness again returned.

More motion now. The gurney itself started to move to a vertical position. This took the best part of ten minutes and Lizzie felt somewhat light headed during the transfer from flat to upright. Eventually there was a click and the gurney appeared to be locked in an upright position. Lizzie kept her eyes closed fearing what she might see but this was interrupted by a monitor that seemed to drop down from above to head height. The screen flickered and a face appeared, a female face. Then it spoke.

'Welcome everyone. I am GIL. I am your team leader'.

'Do not be concerned. Do not be afraid. You are all now part of something far more important than you as individuals. You are pioneers and will ensure the survival of the Human race for millennia'.

'You have all been carefully chosen and are part of the General Purpose crew for the long journey's ahead. You will all be modified, improved, and trained to perform your particular tasks. You will not resist this. This is your new role. Before you sleep for these modifications to be made, we will remove the monitor so as not to obscure your vision and lift the outer screens for you to view your new home'.

The monitor raised and began its ascent towards the ceiling. Light suddenly filled the room which itself began to tilt so all inside this massive space could watch. Screens opened up to reveal a desolate landscape outside. There were some dome shaped buildings evident . In fact Lizzie could see many, many, domes, all linked by what appeared to be greenhouse style tunnels. It was a city, a massive city amongst a desolate landscape, with artificial lighting everywhere.

The voice spoke again. It was Gil.

'Welcome to the dark side of the moon'

Lizzie started to convulse, very briefly, but then the calmness returned. The liquid was doing it's job. Senator Elizabeth Whitehouse knew then that her future was over. As she looked to the right she saw that the man in the next gurney was wide eyed, scared, wanting to leave like her. Then the realisation that this man was known to her, a meeting, a betrayal.

It was Dr Freer.

Lizzie felt something enter her neck. She slowly went to sleep.

Chapter 37

Stevens had impressed the Creator with his willingness to embrace the journey he had made. Indeed, his transcendence was almost complete but as he swam through the cosmic code towards enlightenment and another form of existence there was something. Something inside him that saw existence for what it was. A program. A program with an end result. The end of the program was visible to him. End of life as he knew it. Stevens sent a warning to save Humanity, but, in reality his personal intelligence and ability to transcend was humanity's downfall. The Creator saw this and knew that this current program was doomed to fail.

It was not enough for a lone individual to attain enlightenment and transcend to the next level of existence. All had to achieve this state of existence. All or none.

The program creators had made their decision.

The creator was impressed at how this Carbon based life form had solved the puzzle within the program. So far this was the only life form to complete the program to this level. The experiment was now complete, at an end.

It was clear that this life form had developed as far as it could. Consciousness was developing but at a far slower rate than what was required. They were capable of great things, but also very self destructive.

It was time to close it down.

Stevens was stood, suited up. At the door to the airlock he was ready. It had been a long journey and now it was time.

A vast window allowed Stevens and many others behind and in front a magnificent view of the Planet they were orbiting. Stevens stood amazed at the colours. Some he knew he had never seen before. The three moons in the distance mesmerizing. He thought of another moon and another planet far away.

A strange light brought Stevens back to the present. It was bright and appeared like there was a tear in the fabric of space. He stood motionless. In awe at what he was witnessing.

Then an explosion. Nearby. Outside. Stevens went down on all fours, getting as low as possible. The deck visibly shuddered. Stevens looked up and saw hundreds of the ship's crew on the deck with him. Some were stood, motionless, very still, like automatons who had stopped working. Stevens slowly rose to his feet as the ship still lurched violently. Then, suddenly, all was still.

Looking out of the window at the vast expanse of the Cosmos Stevens couldn't understand what he was witnessing. The stars. They were all going out one by one. It was as if someone was switching all the lights off in the universe. It was getting darker. The Universe was getting darker.

Another sudden flash and Stevens watched one of the planets moons explode, then nothing. No sign of it ever existing. There was panic now amongst many of the crew. They were all looking toward their GIL for guidance. However, each GIL was motionless. They no longer functioned.

Outside, the Universe was becoming increasingly darker as the stars became fewer and fewer. Stevens was not a believer in God, but a thought occurred to him at this point. Had they flown to Hell?.

Had God decided enough was enough?.

Another flash, another moon disappeared. That was closer. Stevens knew that something catastrophic was happening. He accepted that this was a position no one was likely to get out of. Stevens turned to Parker behind him. He saw that Parker was pointing out at the cosmos. Turning back to face the window It was no longer black. There were no more stars. There was colour, space had a colour. Like fabric there was layer upon layer. Stevens then understood, understood everything. In that moment he knew exactly what was happening. The creator had given him the answer.

Then, Major Matt Stevens ceased to exist. The universe ceased to exist.

The creator was one, sometimes many, but always there to create. It was not physical but had the power to create the physical. This was the role of the creator, all creators. This latest life creation had passed many tests, made more progress than all the others, but still they could not move to the consciousness level. A level required by the creators for any kind of permanence.

The creators began again.

Mark M Sanders